BYE-BYE BABY
ON THE
Treetops

Elizabeth Muir-Lewis

authorHOUSE®

AuthorHouse™ UK
1663 Liberty Drive
Bloomington, IN 47403 USA
www.authorhouse.co.uk
Phone: 0800 047 8203 (Domestic TFN)
       +44 1908 723714 (International)

© 2019 Elizabeth Muir-Lewis. All rights reserved.

No part of this book may be reproduced, stored in a retrieval system, or transmitted by any means without the written permission of the author.

Published by AuthorHouse 08/16/2019

ISBN: 978-1-7283-8860-1 (sc)
ISBN: 978-1-7283-8861-8 (e)

Library of Congress Control Number: 2019911351

Print information available on the last page.

Any people depicted in stock imagery provided by Getty Images are models, and such images are being used for illustrative purposes only. Certain stock imagery © Getty Images.

This book is printed on acid-free paper.

Because of the dynamic nature of the Internet, any web addresses or links contained in this book may have changed since publication and may no longer be valid. The views expressed in this work are solely those of the author and do not necessarily reflect the views of the publisher, and the publisher hereby disclaims any responsibility for them.

Chapter 1

OK, I should have hurried past. But come on—could I have known that my life would change? No bells rang. Nothing came to worry me. "Glory to God, Jean, did you not sense something?" I could hear my Irish godmother say. No, I didn't. Why on earth would I?

Turning into the old strangely familiar road, I saw the same bungalow standing well back from the road. On my left was a big grey building advertising "Fine wrought iron for sale." I didn't remember that. The farm opposite seemed deserted. Just a soft lowing of cows from their stalls said it was still in business.

I'm a town girl by choice. Being back was a shock. Why? I'll tell you. It was the silence, as if humans had gone, leaving just a whisper that they were ever there.

After about a mile, I came to the entrance to our drive, leading to the house. Two cottages on my right lay beside a steep hill where my sister and I would push our cycles up to Sunday church, held in a hut near a farm where the farmers and their wives gathered. Two old posts still stood on either side of the entrance. The oak tree still had the same notice board hanging off its nail, the names now faded into nothing.

Bumping over ruts and stones, I continued up the driveway. Sheep in the field looked up as I passed. Then, round a bend, there it was—our old home. It was a tall, gaunt building, almost black against the sky. Looking at my watch, I saw it was nearly midday, the hottest time of the day. My dress stuck to the car seat as sweat ran down my back.

At the base of a wall, poppies stood out, splashes of deep red in the shadows. Parking my car in the shade under a tree, I slammed the door, locking it instinctively. Goodness, it was sultry. The air was moist and heavy, with silence all around me. Even the birds no longer sang. Looking up into the branches, I saw sunlight filtering through the leaves. A sudden wind turned them into frenzied patterns of dazzling light.

Bye-Bye Baby on the Treetops

In a strange way, seeing where I had been as a child, I felt like a little girl again, not a thirty-eight-year-old grown woman. I was transported by time, as if the years had never been.

I walked on. Across the courtyard lay the old mill. When I was a child, it had been a noisy, busy place: saws and lathes humming, hammers thudding, men shouting.

Now, there was only silence. Gaping holes yawned in the roof. Broken logs lay where they had been thrown long ago, just visible among the nettles and weeds. Decay lay in the deathly quiet, like the pall of time stopped.

The mill door was ajar. Should I go in? Memories, half forgotten. Two little girls dancing in the shadow of the mill, while in the doorway, a man watched. The mill boss? Why did he watch? "Be nice to him," Mother would say.

We never would. Not with his red face and hands reaching out to touch. We didn't like him, not one little bit.

I went on, but I had to watch my time, as I must go down to the river, my river, or so I thought then, where I sat and played for hours—the passing of the flowing waters my orchestra, dreaming, watching the stream meander past.

Finding the path, I heard the familiar roar of foaming water from the weir. The sun glinted and shimmered through the trees, creating kaleidoscopes of fragmented dancing lights. Looking up, I shaded my eyes. I caught sight of something high up, almost lost to sight among the thick branches. *My God, it can't be*, I thought. It had to be, though. It was the swing my father put up for my sister and me one summer, where Elizabeth and I would sit and dream. After so long, it had grown upwards with the tree and was now so high I could only just see it. Would "Elizabeth" and "Jean" still be carved into the seat? I'd never know. And I had to go, as it was a long journey back to London.

Chapter 2

Bye-Bye Baby on the Treetops

He knew what was wrong with him. Always had. He saw it in people's faces—the horror, the disgust.

But he'd learned to live with it, long ago deciding to make the mill a refuge from the world outside.

Today, with the winter over, it felt warm for a change. This morning he'd gone out early, catching a trout from the river. He'd have that for supper, something to look forward to.

He fell asleep in the sun that flooded through the window. He awoke with a jolt by the sound of a car door slamming—probably the man in the big house. He sometimes came home early from work. But something was different. He listened. Footsteps coming towards the mill.

No one ever came. He didn't like it one little bit.

Peering over the windowsill, he saw a woman walking towards him. She was pretty, blonde, petite. Looking intently, something in his memory stirred. He knew her somehow. But who was she?

No, surely not! He recognised her. He couldn't believe it. After all this time? He slipped onto the floor. Sweating and trembling, his heart pounded. Why was she here? What if she came in? What would he do?

Peering out the window again, he saw her standing there looking undecided. He looked around desperately. Where could he hide if she came in? Then he saw her turn and, with a smile, walk on down to the river.

He slumped onto the floor again. He couldn't move. Why had she come back? He had to know.

The man got up and went outside. He guessed she would go and find her old places by the riverbank. Then suddenly there she was, meandering along the river path, looking up into the trees. She had spotted the old swing.

Longings he thought forgotten arose as he watched— old fears and terrors. But she'd grown up well. That he could see. And one thing he knew: his peace, such as it was, was gone forever.

Chapter 3

Bye-Bye Baby on the Treetops

When I was eighteen, I went to London to study music.

The decision about what I wanted to do was easy. Mother bought me a flute for my tenth birthday. Just as a hobby, she thought, but I was hooked straightaway. My flute and I became inseparable.

I had a good teacher. Soon I was her top pupil, winning prizes, playing in local festivals. Music made me happy. I was good, so no contest.

London was exciting, student life challenging. And I was lucky. As soon as I left college, I was asked to join a top orchestra as first flute. Guess I never looked back.

Now I sat in an underground train on my way to rehearsal. Hurtling miles underground, we were like earthworms criss-crossing the darkness. A train passed in an explosion.

Times had changed since I was a student. People were wary these days. They avoided eye contact. There was fear in the air.

My station arrived. After pushing and shoving up the escalator, we emerged out into the daylight. A hazy sun warmed my face after the cool darkness of the station. I closed my eyes. It would be good to be back by my river.

"Get a move on, dearie," a voice behind me said. "We ain't got all day."

Chapter 4

Bye-Bye Baby on the Treetops

He'd lived in the mill for so long that he never saw the emptiness, the dripping roof, and the rusty machinery lying in the sawdust where it was thrown long ago.

There was just silence, a heavy, overwhelming silence. Only the sound of the wind in the trees and the rushing of the river reminded him of a life outside. Sometimes when the solitude became unbearable, he banged his head in frustration against the walls, especially during the long dark winters, his shouts echoing round the room.

He never saw anyone. No one ever came. No one knew he lived there. He made sure of that.

Every so often, he hitched a lift to London to do a bit of burgling. That was all he knew. Last time he was caught. It took three police officers to handcuff him. He was thrown into a place where everyone seemed mad and told him he was a menace to society.

He wasn't stupid. It didn't take him long to see that they were the idiots, easily conned. "Yes, I'll take my medicine. Yes, I'll behave. Yes, I'm sorry. Yes, I feel less violent." They were lies. If anything, he was worse. But they let him go, on probation. After that, it was easy. He just disappeared again, back to the mill.

He had no illusions. He knew what was wrong. Was he mad? He felt mad.

After seeing that woman the other day, a paralysis gripped him. Torment and sick despair made him want to kill, purge his hate, anything. He paced day after day, up and down, muttering, voices hammering in his head.

One morning he came face-to-face with a broken piece of mirror leaning on a shelf. There, in the chipped glass, his image glared out at him. With a scream of rage, he smashed it into pieces that fell to the floor.

Exhausted, he sat down. He must do something. Anger was eating him up inside. He'd read the paper, have a mug of tea … anything.

He picked up the local paper and turned the pages. He

didn't read very well; he usually just looked at cartoons or photos. Then, on the third page, covering the arts, he saw a photo. The caption read, "International flautist in concert." He looked closely. It wasn't a very good photo, but it was her, no doubt! Short blonde hair. He imagined her hair down to her waist. Pretty, very pretty. How like her mother she was. How long? Must be twenty years. She'd be in her late thirties now.

"So you're famous, are you?" he asked the photo. As he devoured it, a plan, an idea of how to find her, came to him. Something ugly took shape, something that had been waiting so long.

Chapter 5

We all want to be what we're not, I guess. I, for instance, would like to be tall and dark. The reality? Short and blonde.

I hate my snub nose. No amount of pulling every night when I was a teenager brought any improvement. I have a full mouth, great for flute playing, but in my eyes, not a good feature.

Men's opinions seem to differ. "A great kisser," a lover once said. "Bridget Bardot to the life," maintained another. Oh, come on, chaps, get a life! It gives you the picture, though.

I think I've already told you that I have a successful professional life. I travel the world. In fact, I've just returned from a tour of Australia and New Zealand. I teach when I can as well as play in a quartet when I can get time off from the orchestra.

So yes, I was lucky. "Not luck," my revered teacher would splutter. "Just bloody hard work."

True. But luck is in there somewhere, being in the right place at the right time.

Not so lucky with my love life, though. Married for a while. A disaster. I did try—honest. But maybe that was the problem. Should I have to try so hard?

There was a horn-playing lover after that, ending in mutual relief. I couldn't live with his obsession with clearing up. He found my somewhat forthright opinions annoying. I don't think I'm bossy, but I suppose I am. A dreamer too.

I'm not dreaming now, though. Something odd is happening, nothing I can put my finger on. Just a feeling of being watched ... I tell myself it's my imagination, that I have been watching too many detective films.

But then there are the phone calls. They're real all right, every morning on the dot of nine. When I answer, there's nothing—no deep breathing, no sound. Someone's there, though.

This morning I had had a rehearsal in town, so I decided

Bye-Bye Baby on the Treetops

to come back to my house to relax before the evening concert, put my feet up and have a cup of tea.

As I reached my house (a mews two-bedroom tiny house on a fairly busy street), a van drew up just as I was opening the door

"Ms Turner?" the driver called. "Flowers for you. Please sign here."

They were roses. Carrying them in and picking up my post, I took them into the kitchen, putting them in the sink.

Who could they be from? I had no birthday. No current boyfriend. No important concert. A card lay among the blooms. It was a black-edged funeral card, nothing written on it.

Great. Someone's idea of a sick joke.

Throwing it in the bin, I made a cup of tea and a sandwich, took my shoes off, and with relief sat down on the sofa.

The letters were mostly bills, but there was a contract from my agent as well as a letter from my sister Elizabeth, who lived in South Africa with her family. I'd keep that to read later.

And there was an odd one, unstamped. Must have been delivered by hand. The writing was childish and unformed …

Opening the envelope, all I saw inside was a small photo of two people, nothing else. They were standing hand in hand, a man and a woman, the woman leaning towards the man with a smile. They looked like lovers. Behind them was a building which looked familiar. So did the couple. But the photo was old, cracked, and yellowed by time.

Getting out a magnifying glass, I looked closely. The woman was my mother, the mother of my youth. The man was the mill boss, the one my sister and I had not liked.

I was stunned. My mother! That man! Standing like lovers … And that smile. Surely not?

Elizabeth Muir-Lewis

I sat until the light grew to shadows. Then the clock chimed six. Shit. I had a concert tonight. I would be late.

Changing into concert gear and dashing out, I found a taxi and reached the Festival Hall with barely ten minutes to warm up.

And tonight, just when I needed total concentration (I not only had Mozart's flute concerto to play, but the Cimarosa double flute concerto as well), all I could think of was Mother's smile as she leaned towards that man.

With just enough time to gulp a cup of coffee, we were on.

Calm is what a player wants. I was not calm. I was in turmoil. But I hadn't been playing for so long without acquiring a solid technique. I sure needed it now. And wonder upon wonder, the sound was steady. I played well, extremely well.

After the interval, I had the Cimarosa double flute concerto with Michael, the second flute. It was the second to last item, so I could do a bit of audience spotting.

There was the *Times* critic in his usual place, scribbling. I spotted a friend in the third row, who gave a thumbs up. The front row had a mix of students (they were the ones with scores) and quite a few regulars.

Letting my gaze wander to my right, I could see a man at the far end of the row. He was sitting forwards, a hand covering the side of his face, looking at me, it seemed. No, not just looking—glaring. I must be imagining it. Looking away, then quickly back, it was unmistakable.

My neck muscles tightened. Great! And it was time to play.

I played badly. Damn, damn, blast the man. Who the hell was he?

We finished the concerto. I looked at where he was sitting. He had gone.

I doubt I listened to the rest of the concert ... Then it was time to go out into the night, when it felt safer right now to sit in the shadows. Who was that man? Had I imagined it?

Michael, the second flute, came over. "Hi, Jean. Are you OK?"

"Sort of, Michael."

"Listen, let's go get a drink. I know a pretty good place. You honestly look as though a brandy would help."

I thought about going down the dark street to my house. "Great, I'd like that."

The cafe we went to was not very far from my house. We had taken a bus from the hall. Inside, the room was warm, the buzz of people talking making me feel I was making too much of what had happened.

Michael was talking. As we sat across the table, I looked at him and realized how handsome he was. Why had I never noticed before? After all, he'd been sitting beside me for at least a couple of years.

"OK, Jean. What happened this evening? I know something did."

"You're right. It did. And not just tonight."

"I'm a good listener, if it would help. I'll just say that up until our concerto together, you had been playing like a dream. Then suddenly you were so tense that I could have cut the air with a knife. I couldn't think it was nerves. I've sat next to you too long to think that. All I sensed was that you were really troubled."

So I told him. The phone calls. The flowers. The photo. The feeling of something I couldn't explain. And now ... that man in the audience tonight. "Whether they're linked, I just don't know."

"Could be a crank. You're in the public eye. You're attractive. It's not unknown for some man to obsess about a public figure. On the other hand, the photo seems to make it more personal, something from the past."

Talking about it gave me relief, even if no solutions. We

stayed talking, mostly shop, until all the other diners had gone.

Outside, it was pouring. People ran by under umbrellas. "Here, take my coat." Michael put it over me. We ran, laughing, arriving at my door breathless.

I didn't want him to go yet. "Come in for a coffee."

Over steaming mugs, we talked. Time passed.

"God, it's one o'clock, Jean, and we both have rehearsals in the morning."

"Take my brolly—it's pouring."

Passing me, he leaned down, kissing me on my lips. "There. I've wanted to do that all evening."

So had I. But I didn't tell him.

As his footsteps died away down the street, the taste of his lips lingered on mine.

Chapter 6

wanted to sleep more than anything, but it eluded me. A hideous face glaring. Phone calls. Someone following me. Yet nothing there.

No point in fighting it. I might as well get up and do something—have breakfast, a bit of practice …

It was a dark morning, the sun not yet up. I made breakfast and then read the morning reviews. "Jean Turner, one of our finest flautists, played with her usual mellifluous tone," one of them read.

That was something. He hadn't picked out my bad patch.

Michael got a mention too. He was good. Our sounds went well together.

Washing up, I decided to practice, morning workouts a habit of a lifetime. Without them, I never felt happy. But this morning was a no-go. My lips felt thick, my breathing laboured …

A shower … That would wake me up.

The phone rang. Oh God, nine o'clock. I'd nearly forgotten. I didn't need this. And why did I somehow know that this morning it would be different?

Lifting the receiver, I heard silence, but not for long. Then there was a voice—deep, ugly, northern … "You saw me last night. I saw you looking."

"Who the hell are you? What do you want? Why are you doing this?"

"What do I want? You'll soon find out." The phone went dead.

I'd soon find out? Find out what?

Once again, I forgot time. Once again, I was late for a rehearsal. Another dash, getting there as the orchestra was about to begin. "Sorry, everyone."

I loved rehearsing. But not today. My head throbbed. My mind wandered—images of eyes boring into mine, a voice in my ear: "You'll soon know." Mother smiling into the eyes of a lover …

During the break, I went out onto the steps of the church. In the distance, St Paul's endless cars passed. Crowds … A woman resembling Mother a bit walked by.

Oh, Mother, what is it I should know? What did you have to do with all of this?

Chapter 7

Bye-Bye Baby on the Treetops

Rehearsal was over, and I didn't hang around. Musicians' banter wasn't something I wanted right now. Anyway, I liked to get home to my sanctuary, where I felt safe.

Well, that was an illusion. As soon as I went in, I knew someone was there. My front door goes straight into my lounge. It was in half darkness. Sitting in the gloom at the far end of the room was a figure.

"What the hell?" I reached to switch on the light.

"Leave it!" a harsh voice barked.

My heart thudded. I knew who it was. Silence. A lorry passed.

"How dare you come into my house? What do you want? Who are you? And how did you get in?"

"Easy. I'm a burglar." This seemed to amuse him. He gave a cracked laugh.

Should I laugh … cry? Was I getting hysterical?

I knew that this was the man at the concert last night, the man on the phone, the man who had sent the photo. I couldn't see him clearly, but I knew it was.

And what was I going to find out? Well, if I thought the worst thing was not knowing, what came next made it pale into insignificance.

I sat down. Heavy breathing was the only sound. He was a big man, his bulk filling the space between us. Even across the room, I felt emotion.

He sighed. "I knew you long ago, when we were both children. I watched you and your sister dancing in the courtyard, swimming in the river. I watched you playing your flute, sitting on the bank. My dad was foreman at the mill. Do you remember?"

Yes, I remembered.

"I hid. You never knew I was there."

Hadn't I? There had been times that I sensed something behind me in the bushes. Yet when I turned, it was only swaying grass in the wind.

"What right do you have coming here to frighten me?"

"What right! I'll tell you why—but first look."

I wasn't prepared for what I was to see. Switching on the light, he turned towards me. There in the dim light was a face of terrifying horror—deep scars running up from his mouth to his left eye, his lips pulled into a horrific sneer, a sightless eye distorted ... a face of nightmares.

Did I feel fear? Surprisingly not. Just terrible pity.

He sat down again. On the table was a book. Pushing it over to me, he said, "Read. Learn what made my life a living hell."

I took it. It was a diary, aged from use.

He sat back, one eye fixed on me. Opening it, I noted that the first pages were the usual notes of daily happenings.

Work going well—plenty of orders.

I kept flicking on, not knowing what I was looking for, conscious of that hot eye boring into me.

I got to March of that year.

March 2: New family in the big house. They came over to say hello. Seem nice.

March 5: Today the wife came over. She's called Elizabeth. Said to call her that. Very friendly but seems lonely.

March 10: Elizabeth came over. I let her work one of the lathes. She seemed to like it.

I looked up. That was Mother I was reading about! He didn't move. Just waited.

March 14: She comes over every day now. I'd better watch out. She's very attractive. I find myself looking out for her ... her perfume. Last night I dreamed she was in my arms.

March 17: Oh God, I'm lost. I love her. I didn't mean for this to happen.

I put the diary down. He was still staring. Waiting.

"It was all so long ago."

"It wasn't for me." His eye glared, and that terrible face caught in the light.

"I see that I revolt you. How did I get like this? I'll tell you. Your mother was always coming over, a game to while away her boredom. Not for my dad. It was no game. He waited for her every day. His work was neglected. His men knew he was besotted; he didn't care. I knew. And I saw …"

He couldn't have been more than ten!

"My dad always said I had to go down to the river when she came, but one day I didn't. I hid. He'd turned off the machines. The men had been sent home. I saw them go into the room at the back. I could see in. How I hated your mother—oh, how I hated her. What they were doing …"

I felt sick. What had I expected? Not this—that was for sure.

He couldn't seem to stop now. "Your sister came over looking for your mother. I saw panic. Your mother threw some clothes on, came running out, and took your sister home. I waited until the machines were switched on again and then went in. He took one look at my face. He knew. He shouted, 'Why haven't you obeyed me!'

"I shouted back, 'How could you do this! Don't you love Mum anymore?' I didn't really understand, but I knew what he and your mother were doing was wrong."

I couldn't look at him. His pain filled the room.

"That day I hated him." He paced up and down. "I'd loved him; now I hated him. We were standing by the machines. I could hardly hear in the noise. He was shouting, yelling. He had a foul temper, you know. He pushed me. I slipped, falling sideways onto the machine, right onto the blades. My face was nearly taken off."

"Oh my God."

"Dad drove me to the hospital. My cheek was hanging off. The agony, the blood, the terrible agony ... Sometimes I still feel it. And did he say he was sorry? No. Just drove in grim silence. At the hospital, no effort was made to save my face. It was just stitched up, patched. He didn't care. Why didn't he care?"

The cry of agony from so long ago ... And in the middle of this terrible tragedy, my mother. My beautiful mother.

Almost as if he'd read my thoughts, he looked up. "Don't pity your mother. You know what she did? She left without a word. One day there, the next gone. Broke Dad's heart that did—Mum's too. She knew you know."

"But why me? What have I to do with all this?" Had nothing dawned on me?

"Why you?" I felt his gaze on me. "I'll tell you. Your mother came, played with my dad, then left. I wanted to kill her. In my dreams, she laughed at me.

"Never in my wildest dreams did I ever think I would see you again. Until last week. You came. I watched. You're just like her. I knew what I must do. Maybe she's dead. I hope not. I want her to feel pain when she knows I've killed you."

So far, I'd felt a weird sort of sympathy. Not now.

Coming round the table, he walked towards me. *Talk. Do something* ... Into the silence came the shrill sound of the front doorbell. I got up. He was too fast for me. For a big man, he could move quickly. Grabbing me, pulling me down onto the sofa, he put a hand over my mouth. I could smell fear, sweat, and smoke.

A voice said, "Jean, it's me, Michael."

I was still being held like a vice. Like lovers, we were joined. But this was no lovers' union. This was a dance to my death.

Michael rang again and then apparently gave up, his footsteps dying away down the street.

Come back, Michael ... Please come back.

Bye-Bye Baby on the Treetops

The grip on my throat and mouth relaxed a bit. I'd heard that talking was a good idea when dealing with someone like this.

"Why did we never see you at the mill? Why didn't you play with us?"

"Dad wouldn't let me, said you wouldn't play with a working-class kid." His voice was suddenly like a high-pitched child's voice. He was mad. You can't reason with a madman.

"Of course we would have."

He got up. "I know what you're doing."

"Let's talk about it, work something out."

Too late. With a growl, he threw me back, hands round my throat, squeezing. I fought. I didn't want to die. I tore at his hands. The room grew dark. I was losing. Flailing around, my arm hit the glass bowl on the table. It smashed to the ground. Then there was a voice somewhere in the commotion. *Michael!* The door came open with a splintering crash.

The man, giving a howl of frustration, leaped up, jumping over the sofa. I heard a thump. He'd hit Michael, I learned later, and then disappeared into the street.

"Jean, are you all right?"

"Guess you just saved my life, Michael."

"Well, thank God! I broke your door open, which is now in a mess."

"I'd be dead if you hadn't." I told him what had happened. "You should see his face. It's ghastly. Poor man. And he's mad, which is hardly surprising. It's a ghastly story."

"Don't tell me you sympathise."

"When he was about to strangle me, I guess not. But when I heard his story from when he was a child—and that my mother was part of it … It's a terrible story. I just wish I'd never gone to the old mill again. Then none of this would be happening. All his old anger and hurt seem to have been stirred up."

"OK. Now practical things. You have a concert tonight."

"Oh God, so I have. I can't, Michael."

"Yes, you can. Come on. You're made of sterner stuff than that. So I suggest going to lie down. I'll wake you about six, OK?"

Could I sleep? My throat ached. If I had imagined it, swallowing made it real enough. I dropped off into a deep dreamless sort of void.

Then I heard a voice say, "Tea's up." Michael stood over me. "How do you feel?"

"Like a ten-tonne truck ran over me," I groaned.

While you've been asleep, I've done a sort of Heath Robinson job on your door until someone can do it properly. Plus, you should call the police tomorrow. And now, my lady, concert. I suggest a hotel. You can't sleep here. So let's go find somewhere, have a meal, and I'll stay with you at the concert."

I wasn't used to this sort of caring. It felt good.

I packed all I needed, and we left. We found a room in a small hotel not far from the concert hall and had just enough time for a snack. I couldn't swallow anyway. Then I went to work.

Mind you, I don't know how I got through it. Training, I suppose. By the last bar, I was tired to my soul and pretty sore, with a neck stiff and, I suspected, all the colours of the rainbow.

At the hotel, we had a drink.

"Michael, before I collapse, I want to thank you for everything."

"I'm just glad I got there when I did."

"Amen to that."

I did wonder why he had. Most men would have run a mile. Anyway, whatever it was, I wanted more of it.

"Come and have breakfast in the morning."

"Right, ma'am. How about nine thirty?"

Upstairs I dropped into bed with the last thought before

falling asleep being that I had something to do in the morning. In his hurry to leave, the man had left the diary. I wanted to read it to find out what had happened so long ago, to understand how my adored mother could have become embroiled in such a tragedy. That it was indeed a tragedy, I had no doubt.

Chapter 8

Bye-Bye Baby on the Treetops

Miraculously, I slept, waking at eight. I never could sleep in, however tired or how late I had been up the night before—the penalty of waking in different countries and different hotels on tour.

Getting up, I viewed myself in the mirror. Wow! A rainbow of reds, browns, and dark blues.

After showering and putting on jeans and a sweater, I made a cup of tea with the hotel kettle. Settling down, I opened the diary. Did I want to know more? Not really. But there was no going back. I had to.

The front cover was almost off. Had the man taken it out year after year, reading it over and over, fuelling his anger?

The photo lay inside the flyleaf, where I had put it last night. There was my mother, golden-haired and extremely young. Had Father been away too long? Had she told him lies? What was it the man said—that she had sneaked away without a word?

I found the page where the mill boss (Mother's lover) had realised that he loved her. His name was Charles. The man, his son, was called John. Did it make a difference? I was putting a name to them; they were no longer faceless characters.

What came next chilled me.

> *Elizabeth came over again this morning and told me she would be leaving. She can't mean it. I couldn't bear that. I told her so. God help me. I said that I would rather kill her than lose her. Have I lost my reason? I must have. And John ... I know what I've done to him. Do I feel remorse? I should, but I don't. His looks destroyed ... It's no use. All I can think of is Elizabeth ... Elizabeth ... Elizabeth.*
>
> *So long ago.*

Elizabeth Muir-Lewis

I read on. Two days had passed.

> *Waited for Elizabeth. Waited and waited. Where was she? Could bear it no longer. Went to the big house and asked if they knew where she was.*
>
> *"Oh, she's gone, Charles. Left this morning. Gone to join her husband. No forwarding address, I'm afraid …"*
>
> *Gone! Gone! Without a word. How could she? My love, my love …*

It tailed off down the years, the ink long faded, the cry of a man in agony. Was this the beginning of the tragedy or the end?

One thing I had to know: why did Mother leave without a word?

Chapter 9

The diary kept me totally absorbed until I heard a knock at the door. It was nearly nine thirty. I'd been reading for over an hour.

Opening the door, I saw Michael leaning against the doorjamb. "Breakfast, madam," he said as the grinning waiter carried in a large tray. "Eggs, melon, toast. and coffee."

"Just what I needed." I kissed his cheek.

The waiter set the table, leaving with a wide knowing grin.

"Mmm ... colourful," Michael said, looking at my bruises.

"I can at least swallow this morning. Must look pretty awful, though. You're a brave man."

"Guess so," he said, dodging a thrown napkin. "Anyway, the day has started well with a kiss. So let's dig in; I'm starving."

After coffee, I told him what I had learned from the diary.

"My God, your mother really got herself into a fix."

"She sure did. That she led the man on seems certain, but I honestly would think that she did it innocently. If you met her, you could guess that. And I remember something about the boy—that man called John—how he never seemed to have any friends and would run away whenever he saw us. That same boy has grown up to be a violent, bitter man."

"Listen, Jean. You must go to the police. I might not be around next time."

He was right, of course. But what could I tell them?

"I'd rather wait. After all, I may never see him again. You know, Michael, I've never come across anyone so lost—someone society missed. The system failed him. And knowing the story—and that terrible face."

"I do believe that you actually sympathise with him. He did try to kill you!"

"I know. It's illogical. But honestly, if you'd seen him, heard his story, you might feel the same."

"Somehow, I don't think so, but OK, I won't press you ... So let's talk about something else. I've come to make you an offer you can't refuse."

"What? Tell me."

"I play regularly with a chamber orchestra [he named an orchestra I knew of], and we're off to Sweden to play in an opera season. Our manager called this morning. We've lost our second flute; she's taking time off to have a baby. I've suggested you."

"Where in Sweden. Stockholm?"

"No, Drottningholm, not far from Stockholm."

"Isn't that where the orchestra plays in period costume?"

"Yes, they do. It's a small baroque theatre in the king's summer palace."

"So when is this, next year sometime?"

"In three weeks, actually."

"What! I couldn't, Michael. I've got concerts, recitals ..."

"Yes, you could. Get some stand-ins. Anyway, I've got totally selfish intentions. I'd love if you could, and the manager sent a message to tell you he would be very keen."

Of course I wanted to go. But how? Looking at my diary, I worked it out that most of my bookings were orchestral. "Listen, Michael. I would love to go. I've heard about this theatre, and it would be something different." Plus good to get to know him better?

Time to pack up and get home. I had my door to organise. Phone the police. Speak to my manager ...

It was a relief to find that my house hadn't been broken into. If only a thief had known how easy it was. A locksmith came over, suggesting a numbered lock. "Slows thieves down. They don't like that."

Telling him to get on with it, I spoke to my manager as well as contacting some students to see if they could cover for me. My agent said he would set up a contract with Michael's orchestra. "It's a fine orchestra, Jean."

The new door lock was in place. I felt happier knowing it was up to date. It didn't stop my heart from beating a bit faster, though, when I went back in or from jumping when the phone rang. The nine o'clock calls had stopped; that was one thing. I had phoned the local police, but no one had come so far. And this man ... What else was he planning? I didn't think he would give up.

Michael's orchestra manager rang. "It's great that you might be free to join us. Absolutely delighted, Jean."

My agent thought there were no problems.

I had two weeks and three days to get ready, and apart from some recitals and one orchestral concert, plus some coaching's at the academy, I had time to go shopping, which of course called for some new clothes ... a new hairstyle ... a new lover?

And when I got back, I had something to do: go see my mother.

Chapter 10

Elizabeth Muir-Lewis

With a last minute push, I was ready.

I met up with the other members of the orchestra at London Airport. The orchestral world is a small one, so I knew quite a few of them. The leader, Marion, was new to me. A large full-bosomed noisy woman with a generous, friendly personality, her booming voice reverberated round the airport.

"Great to have you, my dear. Damn nuisance when Mary waltzed off to have a blasted baby."

Margaret, the second horn, was the antithesis of Marion, a shrinking violet with horn-rimmed glasses and tight red curls, very quiet and prim. Marion obviously terrified her. I smiled at her, and like a little puppy, she latched on to me.

After a bit of hanging around, our flight was announced. I had a window seat next to Michael. I didn't tell him I had a problem, that I was a member of the White Knuckle Brigade. The thought of hanging in the sky with nothing but miles of nothing between me and the ground brought me out in a cold sweat.

The plane rolled off. I closed my eyes. *Keep them shut*, I told myself. *Don't think about it.* Easier said than done. *Think about where we're going.* The little baroque theatre was built by a king for the queen he loved, who died, and the theatre was closed for two hundred years, until rediscovered.

I fell asleep. I dreamed.

I was standing outside an extremely low door. To enter it, I had to bend down like Alice in Wonderland, into a ballroom ablaze with lights from magnificent chandeliers. On the walls, paintings and rich curtains at the windows looked out over parkland.

On another wall, there were huge tapestries of woodland dancers, who, as I looked, began to move, to dance, twirling faster and faster, their satin and silk costumes glinting in the light, painted rouged faces grotesquely grinning. I could hear laughter as they looked out at me, sharp teeth bared, long pointed nails clutching at each other.

Backing away in terror, I bumped into something behind me. A voice whispered, "I'll kill you. You won't get away again."

Turning, I saw John standing there, his face near mine, those terrible scars burning in the light.

"Wake up, Jean."

"Oh, Michael. I had an awful dream."

"I could hear you moaning. And am I right—you don't like flying?"

"No, I don't. Never have. Pathetic, isn't it?"

As we came down to land, my heart rate returned to normal.

A man was there to meet us. We were led to a bus to take us to Drottningholm. I made a decision as we got on board. I would put everything aside and enjoy this unique trip.

Drottningholm is an island, so went over by ferry to our hotel, a lovely old place. My room was on the first floor. Michael's was on the same side, one floor up. He carried my bags into my room.

"Spoiling me, sir," I teased.

"Guess so. How about dinner? The players like to get together, and you can get to know everyone."

"I'd like that."

"See you around six in the bar, then."

My room was enormous, with a vast double bed in the centre. I had a balcony looking out over the water, with forests and hills in the distance.

At the foot of the bed was an ancient oak chest. A wonderful wardrobe was up against a wall, and next to it were lithographs of old Drottningholm, telling how the palace had been given to Queen Louise Ulrike (sister of Frederick the Great).

I also learned that the area where we were to perform still used the original stage machinery. Now that would be interesting.

Before meeting up with Michael, I unpacked and settled down to practice. After an hour of hard blowing, I then decided to bathe. I was putting bath salts into the great old bath when the phone rang. Lifting the receiver, I heard a voice ... *Oh my God!*

"Thought you could get away, did you? Not far enough ..."

Slamming the phone down, I thought, *How on earth could he have found out where I am?*

Without thinking, I dialled Michael's room. "He's here. The man's here."

"I'll be right down."

He must have run. I opened the door and fell into his arms.

"He's here. I can't believe it."

"How do you know he's here? He might have been ringing from England."

"No, he's downstairs. I just know it. Voices in the background were speaking Swedish, I'm certain." I went over to the window.

"Michael, I have to face it. I've got a stalker. And why? Because of something my mother and his father did. Because of what happened to make him loathsome, he wants to kill me. And whether I like it or not, I'm bang in the middle of it all."

"Listen, Jean. We're here to do a job, and I'm here. I just hope you're wrong. But whatever, it has to be faced. By the way, do I hear a bath running?"

I dashed into the bathroom. "Just in time."

"Let's have a cup of tea and you can bathe after."

Somehow, he made things seem normal.

In the lift down, I could not stop thinking how everything had changed. One telephone call and my peace of mind destroyed. A sick maniac hiding in dark shadows wanting to murder me. And damn it all—I wasn't going to let him.

Chapter 11

Elizabeth Muir-Lewis

He'd followed her to Sweden.

It had been so easy to find out where she had gone. The girl in the library had been helpful. And there on the screen was a photo staring out at him.

He sat for hours, devouring her image, oblivious to people staring. The girl came round several times to ask if he was finished. He only had to turn to look at her to send her scuttling away.

There was an agent's number on the website, with a telephone number. He'd phoned one morning. "I'm her cousin," he lied. "I want to surprise her. I live in Stockholm and haven't seen her for ten years."

The manager gave him the name of the hotel and the theatre where she would play. Just one problem: he had no money. So he stowed away in the back of a lorry leaving from Dover, getting to the port in another lorry. It was a long, tedious journey, with nothing to drink or eat. When he dodged out of the lorry when it arrived in Stockholm, he was dirty and starving. How to get to Drottningholm?

In the toilets, he cleaned up as best he could, then thumbed a lift on the motorway. Lorry drivers ask no questions—just glad to have company. If the driver was curious, it didn't seem to worry him. Perhaps he was used to it.

He hadn't expected a ferry. The lorry was going over, so he just stayed on.

When the orchestra bus arrived, he was waiting. He saw Jean get off the bus and go into the hotel. A man was with her. They were laughing. Had a new one, did she? Feeling safe, was she? He'd soon change that, wait until she was settled, feeling relaxed, thinking he was far away. Wouldn't she be surprised when she heard his voice! For that's what he planned to do: ring her.

He walked into the hotel, looking around for a house phone. People stared. With his crumpled clothes and unshaven face, he looked worse than usual. Guests saw him, moving away as he walked towards them. It wouldn't be long until he would be thrown out. He must be quick.

Asking for Jean's room number with an underlying threat in his voice, his one hot eye glaring, the girl behind the desk seemed too terrified to refuse.

"Room five, sir."

There was a phone in the corner. When he dialled number five, Jean answered, sounding happy, then panicked, slamming down the receiver. So far, so good. He'd created fear.

He saw the concierge walking towards him. It was time to leave.

Outside, night would soon be here. In this northern land, it was cold when darkness came. He could wait. It might be hours, but he was patient.

At last, he saw her emerge from the hotel with a group of people. They were laughing at something. He didn't like that. Obviously, he hadn't frightened her enough.

By now, he was frozen and hungry. He slunk away into the shadows of darkness.

Chapter 12

Bye-Bye Baby on the Treetops

This morning we were to meet our conductor, Torbjorn. We had been told that he was very young, with an already big reputation. "You'll like him," the organiser had assured us. Like most musicians, who are generally cynics, we would reserve judgment on that!

He was waiting for us when we arrived at the hall for rehearsal. he certainly was young—not more than twenty-four, I guessed. In fact, he was twenty-five.

I rather liked the look of him—skinny, with blond hair hanging over his eyes, which were an intense blue. And he didn't mess about. There was a short welcome in fractured English, and then we began.

The opera we were to play was Mozart's *Zauberflöte*, a work I had played many times. Players work with all kinds of conductors—some good, some terrible, and a few who have the gift of making a player feel it's all worth it. I began to suspect that here was one of the latter. He drove us hard. As the music unfolded, I felt excitement rising. And I knew I wasn't alone. Among us was that palpable sense of something special, that here, maybe, just maybe, was a master conductor.

This man was someone of few words. He didn't need to shout to get what he wanted. It was as all done with charisma, musicianship, and a baton technique that was clear and decisive.

Lunchtime came. "My friends," Torbjorn said as the rehearsal broke up, "I am told you are very good. Today I find it is so. We make great music together."

"Now that's talent," Michael said as we walked back to the hotel.

After lunch, there was another hard session. My opinion didn't change. It felt as if I were playing this wondrous work for the first time. It's not often you can say that.

A long day, though, and what had happened? That ghastly man had followed me … Pressure? What pressure!

"Let's relax, Jean, have a meal, maybe find somewhere to go, like a show. That is, if you would like to."

I could feel his reticence. After all, in a way, we had only just met. Yet in that time, he had come into my life when I really needed him. And I wanted more.

Before we left the hotel, I went to see the orchestra manager. "Tim, did anyone call you before we left?"

"Yes, Jean. A cousin called to say he wanted to surprise you. Hope that's OK."

Well, not really. He shouldn't have done that. But this man was clever, devious, and dangerous.

We went to a show in what looked like a revue theatre. Any other time, I would have enjoyed it. But I fell asleep. My last thought was, *Is he outside waiting, hiding in dark shadows?*

I woke up as it ended. "Michael, how awful of me. I must have dropped off."

"You looked so peaceful that I hadn't the heart to wake you."

On the way back, we found a tiny restaurant, so hidden that if it hadn't been for Michael spotting a light down an alleyway, we would have missed it. There was just one other couple dining.

Seated at a table with candlelight and soft music mixed with delicious food, I felt happy, soporific. Was it this man sitting opposite? Whatever it was, I felt at peace.

Walking back, we passed houses where the whole area seemed to be in bed, streetlamps throwing vast shadows on the walls as our footsteps echoed in the quiet night.

Michael took my hand. We walked without speaking, each with our own thoughts, until, turning a corner, he took me into his arms without a word. "There." He smiled. "How long I have wanted to do that."

"Me too."

He put his arm around me. "Listen, woman … shall we?"

"Yes, let's."

Bye-Bye Baby on the Treetops

The lights from our hotel were just round the corner. "My room or yours?" Michael asked.

"Mine—it's nearer." That's how urgent it felt.

I had a shower. Michael joined me, soaping me, whispering, "You're beautiful, Jean."

My bed was made for lovers. I had had lovers. Why was this different? How far could pleasure go?

Michael was a skilful lover. With him, I felt no barriers, no shyness, no modesty.

After, as we lay together, Michael got up on an elbow. "I should warn you, Jean. I'm falling in love with you."

Was I falling for him too? Was I still wary? Too many mistakes and disappointments …

We talked about our lives, our hopes … I told him about my dreams—my river and a swing in a tree.

"I grew up to the sounds of water too," Michael said. "For me, it was the sea. We lived in a house on a cliff in Cornwall. I slept to the sound of crashing waves, breakers pounding on the rocks. I miss it. So I understand the pull it has."

We lay comfortably silent in each other's arms.

And illogically I couldn't help thinking about a man maybe standing outside this very minute, plotting … Stupid. *Has he somehow got into my mind?*

I slept. Dreamless. Sweet. Safe.

A hand woke me, caressing me. Michael lay looking at me.

"You're beautiful asleep, you know that? How's my girl this morning?"

"She's fine." I sighed, stretching.

"Don't do that," he groaned. "Don't you know what it does to a fella?"

"Show me," I responded with a laugh.

Chapter 13

Bye-Bye Baby on the Treetops

This morning we had our first rehearsal in the theatre. After breakfast, we all gathered in the hotel foyer and then walked over together, through ornate wrought iron gates, where in a huge courtyard, the palace to our left, lay the opera house.

Before starting, we were given a tour, entering a long-gone past. The stage mechanism was just a series of pulleys. One rope brought up, say, a throne, another waves, and with another, trees came down from the flies. At the back were dressing rooms. "Where the singers lived, often with their families," the guide told us. Each contained just a bed, a Swedish stove, and a table.

"That's all?"

"Wonder how they managed with four children. Wait until I hear some of our singers grumbling," I whispered to Michael.

We filed down into a miniscule pit. The singers were sitting on the stage, ready for a sitzprobe (first rehearsal with the orchestra). Wind players are usually at the back of pits, one reason I don't enjoy playing in an opera. It was no exception here. I could just about hear the singers. They sounded good.

It was another hard day, another confirmation that the conductor was exceptional.

After we packed up at five, we got an invitation to join the whole company for dinner. I went to practice. "See you at seven," Michael called, on his way to practice as well.

Soon the hotel would be reverberating with the sounds of strings, brass, and woodwind, all putting in some work, particularly after a hard rehearsal.

I needed a hot bath, as I was stiff after sitting for hours in one position. Dust coming off the stage had made me feel grubby. Looking at my watch, I realized I had two hours to bathe, relax, have a drink, and dress. It was a luxury to get into the bath. It was an enormous antique one, with gold taps and around it mosaics depicting naiads also bathing. Rather erotic. I must tell Michael.

I finished bathing, then dressed. Getting a drink out of the hotel minibar, I went out onto the balcony. It was a clear night. The inky black sky was filled with myriads of stars. A plane took off in a trail of powdery smoke. From a bedroom above me, a violin played, mingling in a cacophony of sound with the music of a tavern below me.

I had a moment of conscious happiness. If the man was below looking up at me, I didn't, just for that moment, care. He couldn't spoil that.

When I went down to join the others, the moment had passed, dark shadows and odd noises making me jumpy. Damn him.

Michael and the others were already gathered in the foyer. "Mmm, sexy," Michael said, whistling.

That made what I paid for the ankle-length dress I was wearing worth it.

"Flatterer," I laughed.

We were led to a restaurant a couple of streets away. It looked as if the entire company was already there. We were introduced to the stage staff, the costume ladies, the soloists. It looked as though it was going to be quite an evening. It reminded me of Glyndebourne.

After we had been given a drink, a stout man took the floor. "Ladies and gentlemen, it is an honour to have you here. We welcome the British orchestra. We hope that you enjoy Swedish hospitality, Swedish food, and Swedish people. This is in your honour." He insisted that we eat the crayfish on the tables with a drink that I thought was rather strong.

"Come on, Michael. Let's try it all."

I'd done some research on Swedish customs—the ghouls, goblins, Christmas tree, Father Christmas, the yule log ... But the food was an unknown.

Soon we were all digging in. Musicians are notorious

for having large appetites, and I doubt we disappointed. Plus, we were now rather mellow, as time was catching up with us.

"Boy, am I tired, Michael."

"Me too. Let's go back."

"See you in the morning."

I fell into bed with just enough energy left to undress. I was asleep in less than a minute.

Something woke me. I opened my eyes. It was pitch-black, with no sound, but someone was there.

Fool! John is a burglar. Would a locked door have stopped him?

I heard breathing close to me, right beside me. My eyes got used to the dark. Now I could see him—a huge black figure. I reached out a hand to put a light on.

"Leave it."

He leaned over me. "You stole my father!" he yelled, almost in my ear.

Oh, great. In his sick mind, I was my mother now.

My eyes got used to the dark. I could see him quite clearly, hands stretching out towards me to do what he'd tried to do once before: strangle me.

He was on my right. I quickly got out of bed on the other side and made a dash for the balcony. Michael was directly above me. Would he hear me if I screamed? He was quick. And angry. I had escaped him once. We reached the balcony together, and he grabbed me. I screamed. I was fighting for my life again. The balcony was narrow. As we swayed backwards and forwards, suddenly he slipped—or had I pushed him? He fell. Almost in slow motion, he went over and down onto the flagstones below, landing with a thud.

At the same time, I heard banging on the door. Running to open it, I saw Michael standing there.

"It was him. He's fallen from my balcony, Michael."

"Thank God you're OK. Take deep breaths."

He held me until my heartbeat returned to normal.

"We'd better go down," Michael said. "I think a crowd is gathering."

Down in the courtyard, people stood looking curious, shivering in the cool night, staring at a dark mound lying in the middle. Was John dead?

The manager came over. "This person fell, I believe, from your balcony, madam?" he asked.

"Yes, he did. Has an ambulance been called? I will explain things when it has come."

"Yes, madam, an ambulance has been summoned, as have the police. The hotel is not pleased that this happened."

That made two of us.

The ambulance came, as did a police car with lights flashing, sirens filling the night air. The manager had an animated conversation with the police officer, pointing over to me.

The officer walked over to me, his body language not encouraging. It said, "I don't like having to get out of bed for such an occurrence." A nervous tic fluttered in his left eye.

"Madam, I am told that this person"—he pointed to John, who was being lifted into the ambulance—"fell from your balcony. Is this not strange?"

I began to tell him.

He raised a finger. "Madam, tomorrow will do. I'll be here at an early hour. Then you can tell me. It is the hour to sleep."

With that, he got into the car without a backwards look, and then there was the sound of sirens dying away into the night.

I spent the rest of the night in Michael's room, curled up beside him.

In the morning, I lay awake thinking. Then I made a decision, one that I knew Michael wouldn't agree with. I wasn't sure I did …

Bye-Bye Baby on the Treetops

The police officer came back early. "It would seem, madam, that this man is wanted by Scotland Yard. I have been asked to keep him until they get here. We will put a guard by his room in the hospital. He is alive but badly bruised, maybe with some broken bones. I have to say that we are not happy that that this has happened."

Well, does he think I was? Here we go again. He's not happy, I'm not happy, and I wouldn't think that John is happy either.

With a last comment, "I do not like that this happened in our quiet town," he stalked off.

Michael heard the tail end of our conversation. "What cheek!"

"You'd think it was my fault. Anyway, at least I know where John is." A thought struck me. "You know, Michael, these people don't know how cunning John is. I just have a feeling that, having met that arrogant police chap, they won't be as careful as they should be." I wish I hadn't been so right …

Over breakfast, I told Michael what I'd decided. "I'm going to the hospital to confront him. It's something I have to do."

"OK, but take care, Jean. Remember what you said …"

As the taxi arrived at the hospital door, I realised something: I didn't know John's last name!

"This person has a badly wounded face," I tried at the desk.

"Oh, yes. He's here," the girl at the desk said after looking up records. "Room nine on the second floor."

Poor John. Instantly unforgettable.

Up a lift. Down a long almost-empty corridor. Another girl sitting at a desk.

"Number nine."

"Yes, the door over there. Don't stay too long."

No questions? No wondering why I wanted to see the patient? And even worse, no guard outside number nine?

Didn't the police officer tell me that Scotland Yard had asked them to guard him?

Well, here I was. Why on earth had I come? What good would it do? Anyway, too late now. *Here goes.*

I pushed open the door, heart pounding, mouth dry. What would I find? Would he leap at me, shout that I had stolen his father?

All I saw as I went in was a figure lying stretched out on a bed on his back. He looked terrible. Falling onto hard flagstones had done nothing to improve his ravaged face. Yet seeing him from this side, I could see remnants of what must have been a beautiful man.

Oh, there I go. That pity again. But he'd been so young. No one had cared. Still a boy, he'd seen passion and tragedy, had seen people turn in revulsion from him.

I sat down on a chair beside his bed. He gave a big sigh.

"John, it's me, Jean."

That was a good start, but I felt a bit stupid ... Could he even hear me?

"I know your name. I've read the diary. I want you to know something. Maybe it will help. I understand your anger that our parents were thoughtless. Yet they couldn't have seen what would happen after so long. John, it's not too late—even now. Let us help you."

He gave an even bigger sigh, coming from deep inside, ending with what sounded like a sob. Were his dreams so terrible?

A nurse put her head in. "Time to go, miss."

Walking down the corridor, I felt like an idiot. What a waste of time that was.

"Miss, miss," a voice called. The nurse caught up with me. "Thought you'd like to know that the man in number nine opened his eyes after you left. Seemed to have woken up."

Has he indeed? I must warn the police. If John was awake, that would be alarming. Didn't they know that?

When I got back, I rang the police officer. "That man

has woken up, Officer. Why is there no guard? I thought it was requested. And don't you realise that he is a crafty and very strong man?"

"Madam, I would suggest that you leave this to the professionals. I'll take note, however, but there is nothing to worry about."

Oh, really! Well, that put me in my place.

Chapter 14

Tonight was the final rehearsal. Like everyone else running up to the last stages, we all disappeared to practice.

Michael and I had more or less the same practice routine—not surprising, as we'd had the same teacher.

"Remember how he would stand on his head, convinced a rush of blood to the brain was good for his playing?" Michael laughed.

"I tried it just once. All I got was a headache."

"A great teacher, though. We're here to prove it, of course."

Before the rehearsal started, there was a check on balance for the singers. These were very young singers, still studying, and Torbjorn's care and awareness of that delicate balance was impressive. It went well. Closeted under the stage, as usual, I could hear little of what was going on above me on the stage. But I heard enough to see that it was going to be exceptional.

The next afternoon, we got to theatre early because we had to put on costumes. We had all sent measurements before we arrived, and the result was pretty good.

I was given a dress in blue silk, with a very low bodice. Marion, a large full-busted woman, wasn't happy.

"Bloody thing!" she exploded, trying to squeeze into her dress. "My boobs will never be the same again."

Margaret was given a demure milkmaid-style dress, perfectly suiting her attempts to be invisible. She still clung to me as her lifeline, which was becoming a bit irritating.

"Stand up for yourself," I said when I saw Marion being bossy.

On the sidelines, I noticed the first cello taking an interest in her. That would probably solve it.

We all had fun, though, doing each others' bodices up, sharing rouge and lipstick, putting on beauty spots.

"Imagine putting this on every morning," Marion commented.

"They would have maids, I expect."

"What would they think of us, though, with our sloppy jeans and sweaters?"

"Probably think how decadent we are while at the same time being envious of our freedom."

The bell went. We filed into the pit.

"Say not a word," I hissed at the men as they took note of the low necklines.

I was watching the audience as they entered. "Michael, look how they walk." The audience was in evening dress. "I never noticed before how evening dress makes people move better."

"I see what you mean. And now that you mention it, these trousers make me walk more carefully, I tell you."

"Idiot."

The opera began. Wondrous music … Could I ever get cynical enough to never hear the genius that was Mozart? And tonight? The cohesion between players and singers was a magic baton that drew the best from us all. This young conductor would soon be on the world stage.

Afterwards, in the bar, there was the buzz of players' adrenalin still running high. Torbjorn joined us. "Thank you all," he said. "Tonight we made music"—he gave that lopsided grin that had become endearing to the women—"and I have come to ask you something."

Silence fell. Something was up.

"Today I have been asked to go to Moscow to play concerts in the Bolshoi and then in Saint Petersburg. So I ask, will you be my orchestra?"

Even a bigger silence …

"Count us in," came a voice.

"Sounds good, but let's think about it," said our manager.

"OK, I'll wait. And thank you again for your superb playing tonight." He left, leaving a buzz of excitement.

"I've always wanted to go to Russia," someone said.

"Me too," said another.

"I've been," said another. "Red carpet all the way."

Bye-Bye Baby on the Treetops

Would I go? I wondered. *Or would the baby have arrived and the mother be back at work?* Boy, was I tired.

"Bed, my lady," insisted Michael, looking at my face.

We lay together. *I could be with this man forever,* I thought as he held me close.

I fell into a dreamless sleep, waking to the sound of a voice. "Breakfast, madam." It was Michael with a tray.

"Do you spoil all your women like this?" I asked, yawning.

"Only the ones I love. Now, rehearsal is at ten—that's two hours to be a lady of leisure. But before I go down, what happened at the hospital yesterday?"

I told him about John, how I didn't think he had heard me … no guard at his door.

"He's crafty. I have bad feelings about it."

So I suppose what happened next shouldn't have surprised me.

Chapter 15

Bye-Bye Baby on the Treetops

He lay thinking what a fool he'd been when he'd nearly got her. Once again, she'd slipped away.

He listened. Took stock. Pretended to be out of it. Groaned a bit. Some men came in and stood around his bed. He couldn't understand a word, except one term that stood out: "Scotland Yard."

That was how the land lay. They were policemen.

Jean came in. He knew it was her, knew her voice. He let out an occasional sigh.

She spoke, saying how things could be different, even now. Too late. He knew. Too much had happened. He opened his eyes as she went out. Feelings came that filled him with some sort of longing. For what, he didn't know.

Could they keep him here? One thing he knew: he couldn't stay around.

He was bruised—nothing worse—and bloody sore, but at least no broken bones.

The night nurse came in to check, drawing the curtains. He waited until she had gone. Getting up to test his leg, it felt bad. He was sore all over too, but he could walk. Getting up, he looked out into the corridor. No one there, just nurses and patients settling for the night. Quiet reigned.

In a cupboard, he found his trousers and sweater and, as luck would have it, hospital overalls. They were a bit small but would do. Slowly and painfully, he dressed.

Then, carefully opening the door, he looked out. The corridor was empty. The night nurse had left her desk, but probably only for a short while. He must hurry. There were voices in the distance and doors banging. Someone called out.

On his left was a door—to the outside? He'd have to risk it. He walked out. Nothing happened. No cries or alarm bells. Limping quickly to the door and opening it, he saw that there were stairs going down. Maybe he'd be lucky.

His leg hurt, but he forced himself past the pain. He'd only have a short time. Holding on to the stair rail, he went down to another floor, another staircase, then the ground level. He went out an exit door into a corridor. One more push and he'd be away.

He saw a doctor walking towards him. Would the hospital gown fool him?

"Do I know you?"

He hit him hard. The doctor fell back to the wall. John ran through the door to the outside. He must hurry. Now or never. A bell went off. That hadn't taken long. They must have found his empty room.

Use the dark. Disappear into blackness. There were bushes all around the hospital. The brambles tore at him. He didn't care. He came out onto a road. Running out, he began flagging down lorries. At the fourth try, one stopped.

"Where to, mate?" He was an English driver.

"The ferry."

"You're in luck. That's just where I'm going."

Somehow, he'd get on board a boat, get back to England. Plan again. Start again.

To stop any questions, he slept.

Chapter 16

I took Michael's idea to heart, luxuriating, staying in bed, having breakfast, showering and dressing. It was only as I left to go downstairs that I remembered that the hotel manager had given me a note last night. I'd been so tired that I'd just put it in my pocket and then forgotten about it. It was still there.

"Madam," it said, "it is with regret that I have to inform you that the man we had in custody has escaped. A watch has been put on the ports, but there are many ways to leave our country. I apologise for not listening to you."

Well, that was rich!

"A cock-up is what it is," Michael exclaimed when I told him.

So John was free to stalk me ... wait for me. I had no illusions that he would stop. I doubted he would stay in Sweden. He would get back to England, take stock, maybe keep quiet for some time, until one day he would appear again. I had thwarted him twice. He would wait.

But I had work to do. I had Handel to help me. That was the next work we had to play.

Rehearsal and performance went well. The orchestra were going to Russia. I had been asked. "The player you stood in for has decided to concentrate on being a mum, so we are really pleased to have you with us."

When I got back, I found the usual pile of emails, letters, and telephone messages. One of them was from my mother, saying she had missed me and asking if I was coming to see her.

Would I ever hear her soft voice the same way again? Would I always see her running to her lover's arms? We never think of parents touched by passion, yet here was my mother, someone who had preached a moral code that my sister and I had grown up with, who had been consumed by a destructive emotion that was reaching into my life. I had to ask her why.

Bye-Bye Baby on the Treetops

"Can I come and see Mother?" I asked the nursing home matron when I rang.

"Yes, my dear. She'll be so pleased."

Would she be? I doubted it. Not this time. But would she remember things from such a long time ago? Last year she'd had a small stroke. Her memory was short. I had to know, though. I couldn't live the rest of my life wondering.

I had a concert tonight. I didn't remember much of it, nearly missing cues, not listening. Nothing made sense anymore.

A sick man wanted to kill me. Mother had a secret kept most of her life. Why did she do it? Had she stopped loving my father? I didn't think so. Well, I would soon find out.

Chapter 17

Bye-Bye Baby on the Treetops

I told Michael when he rang the next morning.

"Don't be disappointed if she doesn't remember, Jean."

"I must try anyway."

Setting out early, I drove down to Sussex, taking a road I had gone down so many times. My little Volkswagen positively purred when I found an open road.

I travelled through Godstone, where the country really began, headed towards Eastbourne, past Alfriston, the Downs towering over me as I drove towards the nursing home at the back of town.

Parking outside, I sat for a while. I wasn't looking forward to it. What would the truth do to her—that her daughter had found out about her youthful fling, her love affair? No, I didn't think it was that. I thought of that man that my sister and I had disliked, his red face and leering laugh. Surely she couldn't have loved him? A love she couldn't talk about ...

A matron answered the door. "Lovely to see you, Jean. She's all ready for you, my dear."

No, she's not. Not this time.

Down the familiar corridor, cloyingly hot. Smells of disinfectant and polish. Murmurs of voices behind closed doors. Nothing ever loud. Even the staff wore soft shoes. No one shouted or banged doors.

I knocked. Mother's soft voice said to come in. She was waiting for me, wearing the pink bed jacket I hadgot her last Christmas. Her hair, once waist long and golden, was now white, twisted into a bun.

She was always easy to talk to. Today I felt awkward, traitorous.

A matron came in with a tea tray. Silence fell. Mother looked at me with a puzzled frown. "Jean, my darling girl, you have something to say to me. I know that expression too well. You always had it when you had something to say that you didn't think I would like."

I never could get away with anything. So how to begin?

"Tell me, Mother, were you unfaithful to Father?" or "Mother, did you sleep with the mill boss?" No, that wasn't the way to do it.

"Mother, when we lived by the river when we were children, do you have any memories of that time?" I probed gently.

"What an odd question. So long ago."

"I went there last month."

"It was a good place for you and Elizabeth. Rather lonely for me, with your father away a lot."

No reaction? No look of guilt? Had she forgotten? Or was there a sudden stillness?

"Do you remember the mill boss and his son John? An odd boy …"

Silence fell. I said no more. Then, my God, I saw tears in Mother's eyes.

"Of course I remember, Jean. The past is often clearer than the present. Old age does that. But I also know something—these are not idle questions."

This was the strong voice of my young mother. The same piercing blue eyes, her head cocked to one side, something she always did when she was puzzled. No going back now. My heart trembled for this beloved person.

I began. She listened, hands clasped on her knee, clenched tightly. I told her everything from the beginning—about John, the diary and what I had read, his accident … All I left out were the two attempts to murder me. I'd said enough.

"Was it all true, Mother, what I read in the diary?"

How I wished it wasn't. I was willing it to be lies.

She shivered, drawing her bed jacket round her. "My poor darling girl. So long ago. But yes, it was true. Your foolish mother. Will you understand, I wonder, when I tell you about that time. No lies, no excuses, even though I was lonely there with your father away so long. Buried down the long drive, nothing to do. You both at school all day. And Charles was attractive. So I began to go over. I know it sounds stupid these days, but I was very innocent, inexperienced.

"I didn't see what was happening. A diversion was all I thought it was, until one day when I realised he was serious, falling in love with me. And worse, getting possessive. Saying he would never let me go. He even threatened me."

She stopped, looking at me with pleading in her eyes. "You say John is a violent man. I remember him as a boy—terribly shy, rather introverted, definitely repressed by his father, who was a bit of a bully. Actually quite a beautiful boy. Then that terrible accident. It was horrific. And Charles didn't seem to care. That was the worst bit. Actually, from then on, he became almost mad. It terrified me. I realised I had to get away ... but how? Then the opportunity came. Your father got a job down south."

"Why did you leave without a word?"

"I'll tell you why, Jean. Because I truly believed that he would never let me go, that he would even kill me. He had threatened to."

He'd written that in his diary.

"I've carried this secret for most of my life. Not a day has passed without questioning whether I could have done things differently. And not being able to tell your father—oh, the guilt. You can't imagine."

Suddenly, I remembered things, such as how I would catch her in tears, never knowing why. Well, now I knew. Didn't I just?

"But, Jean, I could never have known that it would all come back to put you in danger—after so long. And I know you will wonder whether I loved your father. Yes, always. But I was young, unsophisticated. Flattered, I suppose, at first. Weak, foolish. It was excitement, and it was so quiet there."

Deathly quiet. I remembered thinking that.

"I would lie awake at night wondering what to do. Then this chance came. I made up stories to keep Charles from being suspicious. I pretended to be ill, anything not to be near him. Then one morning we left at dawn, leaving no address. You probably remember."

I did, wondering why we had to keep so quiet.

She then did something I had never seen anyone do. Her slender fingers twisted together as she spoke, and suddenly she was wringing them like Lady Macbeth. But this was no blood-soaked woman. This was a guilty, unhappy person facing a past she had thought long dead and buried. Had she paid too high a price?

Going over, I put my arms about her. Tears ran down her soft cheeks. Gradually, she fell asleep.

I left her, telling the matron that she was tired and asking if she would she keep an eye on her. I drove back to London.

Chapter 18

Elizabeth Muir-Lewis

I needed to talk to someone. Michael came over.

"Wow, she sure got herself entangled in a tricky situation," he said after I had told him what Mother had told me. "At least you learned that a violent father bred a violent son."

"She remembered an introverted little boy, but she didn't seem that surprised. What did surprise me was how clearly she remembers."

"OK, let's talk about something else—like eating, drinking, and making love."

"Sounds good. I'll get a meal going."

"Let me go get a pizza and a bottle. You won't want to cook. Go and change into something sexy while I go and buy something."

"I see. Avoiding my culinary efforts, are you?"

"Listen, my lady. I have no gender hang-ups, so get the glasses out. I'll be back in a jiffy."

Over wine and pizza, we talked. We discussed our student days, our mutual teacher.

"Did you know we all had you thrust down our throats, how we'd never be any good if we didn't work harder? What a paragon you were. Clever chap—it worked. We weren't going to let a female beat us to it!" Michael grinned.

"Did he really? Devious. He did exactly the same to me. Put up some chap as an example—a thin-faced gangly boy. I remember glaring at him over coffee. Probably scared the living daylights out of him. But like you, it made me work harder."

"A great teacher," he said. "Then, when I met this paragon, all I could think of was how to get you into bed. I wasn't the only one either. But you were so dignified that I lost my nerve."

"Me! I'm not like that at all!"

"I know that now, my love. Sexy, desirable …"

"More, more. I like it."

"Come here, woman. It's been too long."

Bye-Bye Baby on the Treetops

"Mm, far too long." We fell onto my sofa.

Michael undressed me slowly. We made love tenderly. Desire? Yes. Good sex? Yes. But beyond that, I knew I loved this man.

We slept. In my lover's arms I dreamed. Uninvited. Always my river. Rushing water.

Above me, a swing sways. I'm on a path. Twigs crackle underfoot. Behind me ... footsteps. I don't want to turn. But I must. Two figures. Men. I know who they are. My feet are like roots grown into the earth. They get nearer. Another figure comes up behind them. Mother! Her arms are held out. What does she want? I forgive you, Mother. Is that what you want?

They walk on. I can't move.

"Mother, help me," I cry.

The figures begin to dissolve. Mother's hair turns white. She weeps and then disappears.

"Jean, wake up."

"It was that damn dream again—always the river. It was scary, Michael."

"Hardly surprising. Memories have been awakened. You've learned some pretty hair-raising things about your past, and you do dream very vividly."

After he left, I went to bed. Maybe I'd sleep ... No luck. This time a jumble, finally falling into a disturbed doze, waking with a sense of dread I couldn't explain.

I had a ten o'clock rehearsal. Just as I was leaving, the phone rang. It was a matron from the hospital. "Jean, I'm so sorry. Your mother had a stroke in the night. I think you should come."

Oh, Mother, what have I done?

I called Michael and explained. "Can you fill in for me? I have to leave at once."

"Leave it to me. I'll ring the manager. Take care, Jean."

Once more on the road to Sussex, I was going round and

round in my brain. Had I killed her? Had it been too much? Yet could I have lived my life not knowing?

I have no recall of the journey—just screaming to a halt in the nursing home car park, ringing the bell. Too late. I knew by the matron's face.

"So sorry, my dear. She slipped gently away just after I rang you."

In her room, she lay on the bed, hands folded, her graceful, slender hands ... She didn't seem dead, just asleep for a while. Any moment she'd wake up and say, "Hello, darling. It's wonderful to see you."

It wasn't hard to see how she would have captivated a man. She was beautiful, the old age lines smoothed out in death, a gentle smile on her lips. Did that mean her last thoughts were happy ones or that she had been glad to unburden herself to me? I'd never know now.

That matron came with a cup of tea, that sop to grief. "Your mother left a note for you."

A note! When had she written it? Was it after I had left her?

It came open easily, as if only just closed, and I recognised her spidery flowing writing.

My dearest daughter,

I want you to know that nothing you said or did has brought my death any nearer; I have felt it coming for some time. Don't be sad. I was glad to unburden myself to you. I pray it won't cause you pain. I always loved your father. I was young and foolish, and I paid a heavy price. Give my love to Elizabeth. I'm so proud of you both, my beautiful daughters. I send my love. Judge me lightly when you speak of me, your ever-loving mother.

If I wept, it was in gratitude. She had absolved me, a last act on this earth.

I stayed to say goodbye, then went to the matron.

"We take care of everything, Jean. All you must do is register her death at the office in town. And if you could decide about her things …"

"Can I do it tomorrow, matron?"

"Of course. That would be best. Your dear mother will have been taken to the funeral home. By the way, there is no need for anything else. She was seen by a doctor only two days ago."

I decided to stay down here to get in touch with my sister and have a few days' rest. I needed to be alone. Emotion had exhausted me—what with confronting Mother, her death, John, plus performing. My soul felt extremely weary.

Just down the road, I found a hotel. They had a room available. That would do. That afternoon, I slept dreamlessly. Something had gone from my head; I felt more at peace than I had for ages.

Until something woke me. What was it? I couldn't hear anything, just peaceful nothing. Of course. That was what it was. The quiet of the countryside had awakened me.

And there was something I had to do. What was it?

I sat up. Of course. My sister. She had to be told.

I dialled her number on my mobile. John, her husband, answered.

"Oh Lord, Jean, I'm so sorry. I'll get her. She's in the pool."

I heard him calling. I heard her cry out.

"Not Mother, Jean!" she cried.

"Yes, last night. Could you come over?"

"Of course. We must be together."

I was close to my sister, always had been. We were just two years apart. Living by the mill as children had thrown us together more than most. We did everything together. The swing up in the tree had been our den, our sanctuary, our private place.

"I'll book a flight in the morning."

"And I'll book a room for you here. We might as well stay here until the funeral."

I rang Michael.

"I can do your date, no problem."

What should I do? Fresh air ... That would be a good idea. Getting into my car, I drove down to the seafront. The winds were gale force, whipping at my clothes and hair, the boom of waves pounding the breakwaters. Walking onto the pier, I saw an outline of France in the distance. Cumulous clouds hung like crimson mountains as gulls swooped overhead, crying like lonely children.

I leaned against the sea wall. I could almost hear Mother saying softly, "Don't be sad, Jean."

Chapter 19

Elizabeth Muir-Lewis

After breakfast the next morning, I went over to the nursing home. Mother's room had been cleaned and tidied. She had gone. Now there was only an empty room, little left of the woman who had lived there for so many years.

Her dresses still hung in the wardrobe. Shoes in neat rows. Always tidy.

Beside her bed was a chest of drawers, filled to the brim with books, papers, Christmas cards, pens, pencils .... When I opened the top drawer, several brown envelopes fell out, together with some photos. They were near the top. Had Mother got them out after I left?

Some of them were old. Some were recent. One of me in Paris. One of Elizabeth with her family. One of Father holding Elizabeth by the river. Another of him and me fishing. Then another caught my eye: a little boy looking into the camera, smiling. It was John, I was sure, before the accident. I could see what Mother meant. He had been handsome.

Then there was a photo of the mill. We were in party frocks. In the doorway stood a figure, watching. I hadn't imagined him then.

Another of John. This time no smile. Sullen. Mother's arm around him. Was it already too late by then?

Mother had a particular dress on in nearly all the photos, a dress I remembered; it was flowered, with a white collar and cuffs.

Opening the wardrobe, I saw the dress among other clothes. She had kept it. Going back to the drawer, I took out bundles of letters. Would she mind? Letters are so personal.

One was from Father—a love letter. I looked at the date. It was after they had left the house by the river. Did that mean that he never knew? I hoped so. Would Mother have been happier if she had told him? Was I judging it by today's thinking? So long ago ... These things were not talked about. I couldn't imagine keeping such a secret.

And it forcibly struck me that had I never known her story, never seen those photos, never met John, all these people in the photos would have been strangers. To be thrown away. Nothing to do with me. But I had, and my life had changed because of it.

I took what I wanted and went to the matron.

"Jean, do you want a religious service? If so, can you contact the vicar who does the crematorium, maybe talk to him about your mother? Plus you should choose her casket and all the other things that go with it."

"My sister is coming over from Johannesburg. May I wait until she arrives?"

Back at the hotel, an email was waiting for me: "Arrive at Heathrow at 9 a.m. Can you meet?"

"Can't wait …"

I had an evening to while away. What could I do? I hadn't been at loose ends for so long; it felt odd.

On my way in, I had seen that Bach's *St. Matthew Passion* was on in town. How many times had I played that! Might be nice just to listen.

I booked a ticket and then walked around to find somewhere to have lunch, finding a fish restaurant down a street facing the theatre. Cod and chips. How long since I'd had that! Right by the sea, it should be fresh.

With a cup of tea and a local paper, I settled down to waste a few hours, when a voice suddenly boomed out from behind me.

"Jean? Jean Turner? Is that you?"

As I turned, I saw a woman stand, huge and flowing, with a face that seemed familiar.

"School? The mad one—nearly got expelled!" she exclaimed.

"For pulling a tablecloth off the table with all the dishes still on it."

"Right." She beamed. "Mother was not happy. She had to pay for all those broken dishes. I'd seen a magician do it. Seemed easy."

Always a bit mad, always fun.

"Caroline?"

"Spot on. It's fantastic to see you, Jean. I'm a huge fan, you know. I follow everything you do." She sat down. "Listen, if you've nothing to do, why not come to my house and have tea, meet my old man …?"

Her "old man" turned out to be a distinguished grey-haired much older husband, an eminent biologist with a large twinkle, especially when Caroline assured me he kept a firm hand. I heard about bungee jumping, skydiving, and treks to the Amazon—and when she assured me she didn't think she should do it anymore. "Getting a bit long in the tooth," she said. This brought his eyebrows right up.

I stayed, and we had an early dinner. She decided to go to the concert too.

I suppose I thought that *St Matthew* might be a disaster. It was a big one to tackle. However, it was done well. There was a London orchestra (I spotted one of my students—must remember to tell her to sit up straight), one international singer (Jesus), and a cast of good solid singers.

The music flowed over me, causing me to close my eyes. Modulations and counterpoint, with their order and sanity, were just what I needed. For a moment, Mother's spirit moved through the bars as the magical final chorus brought the performance to a climax.

Afterwards. Caroline and I went across the road for a coffee, leaving with promises of keeping in touch.

Tomorrow I would meet my sister at the airport, and together we would say goodbye to Mother.

Chapter 20

Elizabeth Muir-Lewis

The matron rang in the morning to let me know about the funeral. After a very early breakfast, I set off for Heathrow.

It had been over ten years since I had seen my sister. We spoke every week, saw each other on Skype. But I'd missed her children growing up, missed being with her.

As I waited at the barrier, I wondered if she would be the same. We had so many shared memories. But time had passed. She'd had a life without sharing it with me, except from a distance, just as I had.

There she was. How could I worry? She had the same bouncy walk and the same smile as she saw me. Time became nothing as we fell into each other's arms.

On the road south, we started catching up. Elizabeth chattered. That hadn't changed. She always was the more outgoing one.

I learned that her husband, David, was retiring next year. "Actually, he can't wait, Jean. He's been asked to manage our arts festival, and that means he can get out on the golf course more often."

"Tell me more about the arts festival."

"It's a mix of music and drama. Actually, I was going to see if you would consider going over for some concerts. Wouldn't that be just great!"

"Let's talk."

No mention of Mother. How to go about it? I hadn't made any plans.

Reaching the hotel, she booked in, her bedroom next to mine, with an adjoining door.

"It's fantastic to see you, Jean, even if the reason is Mother. We mustn't let ten years pass again. The kids are nearly grown up now, and with David retiring, we could get over to see you."

"I agree. Let's plan things, but, Elizabeth, I want to ask you something." I was taking the roundabout way to ease my sister into this tale.

"Fire away."

Bye-Bye Baby on the Treetops

"Do you remember when we lived by the river when we were children?"

"Of course I do. Great days."

"Do you remember anything about Mother, what she did with herself?"

"Hmm." She gave me an enquiring look. "By any chance, do you mean her and the man in the mill?"

"What?" I gasped. "You knew!"

"Sort of. I used to notice things without really understanding. It was only later that I began to put things together—how Mother would jump aside if we saw them talking, how when Father came home, she was nervous, agitated. But it's all so long ago. Why are you asking?"

"I'll tell you. Terrible things have happened, with our mother in the middle, things you are not going to believe."

I told her everything. She read Mother's final letter.

"Oh, Jean, this is awful. I just can't believe that Mother could have got involved with that man. I remember him—a horrible red face with a loud voice."

"Me neither. Can you remember the boy?"

"Vaguely. He always ran off when I came face-to-face with him. I came across him fishing one day, and when he saw me, he scuttled away. Very odd, if I remember correctly."

"Well, he's more than odd now; let me tell you." I told her about him, the diary, his story.

"How did Mother get herself into such a fix?"

"She said that herself. Even after so long, I could see that not a day has passed without her wondering why. Plus, I can't help thinking that while we were swimming and climbing trees, Mother was running to his arms. And now I know why she kept asking us to be nice to him."

Elizabeth looked at me. "I'm guessing that you've found it hard to tell me."

"Of course. Here you are for our mother's funeral, only for you to learn about a pretty catastrophic period in her life—and in mine, if I'm honest."

"Where is this John now?"

"Out there somewhere." I told her about Sweden. "Planning how to scare me. I'm his obsession. If you could only take time back. If I'd never gone to see the mill and river again ... *If only* ... I guess life's full of those. That morning, he saw me again, realised who I was. All the agony and the terrible times when he was a boy must have come back."

"Go to the police."

"I have thought of that, but what can I say." Whatever I decided, I didn't want to waste time now that I had my sister here. We went for lunch, and there was non-stop talking and catching up. I managed to put things out of my head. There was nothing about Michael. I was keeping him as a surprise. Elizabeth always worried about my love life.

After lunch, we went to the town hall to get the death certificate, then the funeral home, where a long-faced lugubrious man with dark stubble sat behind a desk in the front office. His voice matched his face—long, with a slightly hollow resonance.

"Ah, the Ms Turners. So sad to lose a mother ... Yes, indeed."

In a room were rows of caskets—straw ones, mahogany, oak, pine ... "Some like the ecological ones and a woodland burial," he intoned. "Then there are the flowers, cars, the newspapers informed. We offer a package to include it all."

We decided together, happy to let them take care of everything.

"Undertaker." Elizabeth shuddered as we left. "They undertake to make our exit smooth. What an awful man. A Viking send-off for me."

"Isn't he? Let's go get some fresh air down on the front."

It was a lovely, if cold, sunny day. Linking arms, we strode out together, walking fast from one end of the pier to the other. Fresh air whipped through our hair. Salt on our lips. Matching stride for stride. Just for a while, I forgot to worry. I had my sister with me.

Chapter 21

We went to see the vicar.

How easy it would have been even just weeks ago to talk about a perfect mother. Now we had to pretend, to dodge certain subjects. Probably our fault; after all, only we knew about that episode in her life. Otherwise, she had led a blameless life and been a good mother.

She had passed into death quietly, a smile on her lips. Certainly no one could guess that passion had rocked her life.

Caroline rang to say she would be there. "Your mother was always so kind."

"Do you remember Caroline?" I asked Elizabeth.

"Vaguely. She was a year ahead. Wasn't she bit potty?"

"Eccentric, perhaps. Interesting, though."

The next morning, the day before the funeral, we had a leisurely breakfast and chatted, still having things to catch up on.

"Telephone, Ms Turner," the receptionist called.

"Hello? Jean Turner speaking."

Silence ... I turned cold. Then there was a voice. Oh my God!

"Gone, has she? I've read about it. Sister back, is she? I'm watching." He was gone.

"Jean, whatever's the matter? You're as white as a sheet!" Elizabeth exclaimed.

"That was him on the phone. He knows that Mother has gone. He knows you are here. How does he know? Oh, Elizabeth, this gets worse and worse."

Elizabeth didn't answer, just stared.

Where was John now? Was he here? Every ringing phone made me jump.

That night, we went to bed with a chair up against the door handle. There were images of John outside, climbing like Spider-Man across the roof, looking in our windows. Every sound, every thud, woke me.

We both looked how we felt in the morning. I decided I would go to the police after the funeral. He couldn't do much today.

But then, I never learn.

Chapter 22

Bye-Bye Baby on the Treetops

When we arrived at the crematorium, there were a lot of people waiting. The chapel was full. I shouldn't have been surprised. Mother was a member of so many things. Her interests spread into music and bridge; she was an ardent WI member and had been the local chairperson several times.

The vicar did a good job. She was remembered as a good woman, valued by many.

She had asked for one of my recordings. As everyone walked out, "Greensleeves" was played.

She was gone. As we filed out, I asked myself if I wished I had never learned about her past. Yes, I did … But the beautiful golden-haired person who always was there for us would be the memory I would hold on to.

I was shaking hands with strangers, smiling and thanking them for coming. They were people we would never meet again. Something caught my eye. It was a man standing at the gates, looking down at me.

It was John. How dare he on such a day! Anger filled me. I ran up the slope towards him. Too late. He got into a car and drove off.

How cruel. People stared as I stood weeping, shaking with frustration. Elizabeth had run after me. She held me. She guessed.

A car drove in at top speed. Michael! He got out, striding over and seeing my tears. "What on earth, Jean. What's happened?"

I told him. Elizabeth stood with what I can only describe as an open mouth. I introduced him …

"I tried to get here in time for the service, but the traffic was impossible," Michael said. "What will you do now, Jean?"

"Let's get home."

"Hey … dishy," Elizabeth murmured as we walked to my car. "Why didn't you tell me?"

"Keeping him as a surprise—that's why."

"Is it serious?"

"Getting that way. You know my record of failure in that area. So far, all the boxes are ticked. He even likes cooking—a plus that is ... Most men run a mile."

"I've got one of those myself," laughed Elizabeth. "He seems nice, very dishy, and obviously he adores you. Make the most of him; men like that don't grow on trees, sister."

Chapter 23

One thing was clear: Elizabeth and Michael were worried.

"You must go to the police," Elizabeth said as we sat round the kitchen table.

"I will. All in good time."

"She should have right from the start," Michael added

"When they wouldn't have believed a word ... After all, he hasn't committed a crime."

Oh, so stalking and trying to murder you don't count?"

They looked at each other. They were infuriating allies now.

"Your sister has a stubborn streak," Michael said.

How could they understand? Or was I too affected by my feelings for this man? He lived like a leper. Anger and violence were all he understood. I knew what they thought. I couldn't blame them. I wished I could hate him. But in spite of being afraid of him, I couldn't change my feelings.

Michael left after dinner. Elizabeth and I sat round the fire in our dressing gowns with mugs of Bovril.

"Mother always made this in the winter. Do you remember?" Elizabeth said.

"And you would make up stories or we'd play draughts."

"Which reminds me ... You asked if I remembered anything more about this John when he was a boy. Well, I have. It was when I came home early from school one day. I couldn't find Mother anywhere, so I wandered over to the mill. I remember thinking it was unusually quiet; the machines were not on, and there were no workers around. Then I saw him crouching under a windowsill, peering into the room at the back of the mill. I called out. He turned, giving me such a look of hatred that it really scared me. Then he ran off. Mother came running out. Remember how neat she always was? Well, that afternoon, her hair was hanging loose and her clothes looked as if they had been thrown on."

"That ties in with what John told me. That was the day

he confronted his father. He had seen him and Mother making love."

"My God."

"And it was the day he fell under the machinery blades— the day he was tipped into madness."

Chapter 24

Bye-Bye Baby on the Treetops

The next morning, I had a rehearsal at the Festival Hall. Elizabeth begged to go. "It's been such ages, and I've missed you playing."

She had been a sort of camp follower when I started, coming with me everywhere, my best critic. It had been wonderful fun too.

After breakfast, we walked to the underground, joining the masses of workers streaming on their way to offices and shops. "I've missed this." Elizabeth grinned.

"Not much has changed, though. Same trains, same dirt."

"But more people. That I can see. Trains used to be half-empty."

"I don't remember so many people. Almost every nationality too."

"Progress, I believe it's called."

So what made me think I was safe down here among the crowd?

A train came, hot, dusty air wafting in its wind as it rattled towards us.

Moving forwards, I was pushed suddenly from behind—not gently but viciously. If Elizabeth hadn't thrown her arms about me and someone behind hadn't grabbed my belt, I would have fallen under the wheels of the train.

"That weren't no accident, lady," the woman said. "Next te me 'e were. Saw 'im push ye."

I thanked her.

"No need, dearie. Glad te 'elp. If I'd seen 'im in time, I'd 'ave wrapped my brolly round 'is ears, I can tell ye. What's the world comin' to? I arsks ye."

I looked back. A man was walking away, pushing through the crowds. He turned. Our eyes met. Shrugging his shoulders, he disappeared.

It was him. Oh my God.

"Come on, ladies. Get a move on."

We pushed on board, and there was standing room

only. Elizabeth was quiet at first, but then said, "Jean, you have to go to the police now surely."

"Give me time."

"What! Time to be murdered, you mean."

She was right, of course. Walking over the bridge to the hall, I knew without any doubt that once again, I could have died. How many lives did I have left? I could see the headlines: FLAUTIST FALLS UNDER TRAIN.

Tonight was a big concert. I had to play the Mozart flute concerto. My agent had let me know that the conductor was recording it next year with the Berlin Philharmonic. I wanted to be the soloist. Once again, I had to shove everything but the music from my mind.

Elizabeth went into the auditorium to listen.

We all warmed up. I checked some awkward corners. Vibrato. Breathing. If my heart was beating faster than usual, who could blame me? Being nearly pushed under a train wasn't an everyday thing. But Mozart was an old friend. Everything flowed quite well.

We broke for coffee, passing the conductor.

"Jean, will you be my soloist for a recording of the Mozart next March with the Berlin Phil sessions in Berlin?"

"Thank you, Maestro. I'd love to."

I'd got it! Most players would give their right arms to play with the Berlin orchestra.

After the interval came the Neilson concerto, another old friend. In fact, it was the very first concerto I played at the start of my career. It rolled along nicely. Now I had nothing much to do. Elizabeth gave me a thumbs up.

I suppose I felt safe sitting there. No one could get at me here—or so I thought.

Looking out into the shaded auditorium, a movement caught my eye at the top of the hall. I had to strain to see, as it was almost dark up there. But it was light enough to see a man sitting. It was John.

Chapter 25

"OK, let's go," I said as Elizabeth joined me after the rehearsal. "We're going to the police." Hailing a taxi outside the Festival Hall, I added, "Scotland Yard."

"What?" gasped Elizabeth.

"Where else? Whether they believe me is another matter. They might need a murder to take some action—mine, for instance."

"Don't." My sister shuddered.

So in we walked to the most famous police station in the world. The expression on the police officer's face as we went in didn't help our confidence. "A couple of ladies about to be a nuisance," his expression said.

"Could we see someone, please?"

"About what, madam?"

"About a possible murder."

He rang a number and then turned to me. "Room seven, madam. Someone can advise you."

Upon knocking on the number seven door on the second floor, a voice told us to enter. At a large desk sat a large man—a grey man. Grey suited. Grey haired. Grey faced. Grey anonymity. Half glasses lodged precariously on a long spindly nose. He rose. "Yes, ladies. What can I do for you?"

We sat down. A deep breath. *Begin...* I told him everything up to today.

He doodled on a pad already full of twirls and squiggles. It all began to seem ridiculous. Was he even listening?

"The final straw was just an hour ago, when somehow he got into the Festival Hall, and that was after trying to push me under a tube train this morning."

"Quite a story." He smiled, which was a transformation, his face lighting up the grey exterior. "Yes, quite a story. So ... what can we do? You have a dangerous stalker. Possibly a killer. But no actual proof other than what you tell me."

I tried to interrupt.

He wagged a finger. "However, we can look at this from a different angle. As you spoke, something jogged my memory. Some weeks ago, the Swedish police informed us that they had apprehended a known criminal, someone on the wanted list, and that he had been stalking and attempting to kill a British musician on tour there. You wouldn't be that musician, would you?

"Yes, I am."

"Well, well. What a coincidence. We have been looking for this man for some time. After the Swedish business, he disappeared again and we lost track. So now I would like you to see some photos so we can decide if we are on the same wavelength."

We went to a room on the same floor, which was full of nothing but computers. "Can you describe him?"

Describe John? Not very difficult.

"So let's see if we can find him. He's badly scarred, you say. Let's begin with disfigured criminals. You must be patient. There are very many."

Images. An endless passing of men, women, and even children. People burned. Knifed. Some hideous. Some sad. But no John.

"How many are there?" asked Elizabeth with a gasp.

"Too many, my dear. And just the tip of the iceberg."

I nearly fell asleep, until ... "That's him!" I yelled.

John stared out at us, his one good eye glaring.

"And quite a one too," the police officer muttered. "This man is a known psychopath. He's violent, and he has killed. Last year he strangled the wife of a gang boss. Evidently, she was having an affair with one of his men. Your man evidently has a hang-up about infidelity. He went berserk one evening and strangled her; then he vanished. Now the underworld is looking for him, as are we. You don't murder one of their own and get away with it."

Now we knew what drove John—not just hate. It was revenge. He was sick ... mad.

The police officer tapped the desk. "We have these

damn budgets, but I believe you are in grave danger, Jean. If we did nothing, I would feel bad."

"So would we."

He grinned, transformation taking place again. "What are your plans right now?"

I gave him my dates for the next few weeks. "Next week I'm at the Edinburgh Festival."

"I'll have a word with the chief of police up there." He looked at me. "I've realised who you are, Jean. We can't have one of our best flautists in danger, now can we?"

"You know my work?"

"Yes, indeed. Not as well as my wife, though. I've been hearing about Jean Turner for a long time—about your sound, breathing, phrasing. She's an amateur player. She'll be over the moon when I tell her I've met you." He rather shyly pushed over a piece of blank paper. "She won't believe me without an autograph."

I scribbled my name.

"Leave it to me, Jean. Any developments, let me know. Here's my number. Anytime. Don't forget."

In the taxi, I felt happier. *Something's being done at last.*

Chapter 26

Elizabeth Muir-Lewis

At the concert, I felt an atmosphere. After the fourth person had asked if I was OK, I realised that rumours were going around about the strange behaviour of Jean Turner.

I was glad to get it over. In the taxi back with Elizabeth, I hardly heard her chatter.

Arriving home, there was a police officer standing outside. "Evening, ma'am." That had been quick.

I was weary and sick to my soul. Elizabeth fussed over me. "Come on. Into bed."

To do what? Have dreams … nightmares?

"Have a sleeping pill," Elizabeth insisted. "I take one on an overnight flight—always knocks me out."

It did help. I fell into a dreamless sleep.

Michael was coming over for breakfast. He rang to say he would be a bit late.

Soon Elizabeth would fly home. She had hardly arrived. It seemed much too short. "I'll come back soon," she assured me.

"You only seem to have just got here."

"I'll plan something. Anyway, maybe you and Michael …?" She stopped.

"Yes, what about me and Michael?"

"Well, for one thing, you could both fly over to us and play in the festival. Then you could get married … I wouldn't miss that."

"Hey, you're jumping the gun, sister."

"He's right for you. You know he is."

"I'll grant you that, but …"

"And dishy. Thoughtful. Adores you. Clever. What more do you want?"

"Well, for one thing, he's seven years younger than I am. He would want a family, and we haven't talked about it."

"If you mean that you're too old for kids, nonsense."

"Oh, come on Elizabeth. I'll be forty in two years' time. Besides, I don't want children. Maternal feelings simply don't beat in this breast. And I don't want to fail again."

She came over, putting her arm around me. "Michael's a big boy. Mature for his age, I'd say. Anyway, he may feel the same. All I can say is to meet things as they come ... and hang in there."

The doorbell rang. It was Michael. Behind him loomed the police officer.

"Do you know this man, miss?"

"Yes, Officer, I do."

Michael's face was a study. "Scotland Yard on the case now?" he joked.

"Yes, actually."

I told him about Scotland Yard and what we had learned about John.

Michael gasped. "He's a real sweetheart. Thank the Lord you decided to go to the police."

"You know, something the officer said yesterday struck me forcibly—that John had a hang-up about infidelity. We know why, don't we? But after so long?"

"That struck me too," Elizabeth agreed. "I suppose seeing his father and our mother the way he did, and only just a kid, must have twisted him."

I sighed. "I wonder where this will all end."

"Nothing is forever, and now that the police are on it, it'll soon be sorted out." She went upstairs to pack.

I looked at Michael. "You've had nothing but turmoil from the moment you knew me. I'd understand if you wanted to call it a day."

"Listen, my love." He came over to sit beside me. "I hear what you're saying, and I know why. My answer is that I am here as long as you need me. I love you, Jean. And Elizabeth's right—it will soon be over."

It was comforting beyond words. I wish he had been right.

Chapter 27

Bye-Bye Baby on the Treetops

I was off to the Edinburgh Festival in two days' time.

That date was usually the highlight of my year. Not this time. For one thing, I wouldn't see Michael for two weeks. And for another, John was out there somewhere. Plus, Elizabeth was going home.

She hauled me off for a shopping spree. "Things I can't get at home," was her excuse.

So we bought sweaters from Fenwick and shoes from an expensive shop in Bond Street. We had lunch at Fortnum & Masons and tea at Harrods, where she indulged in a coat that set her back a few hundreds. "John never minds," she assured me.

I remembered her rather nice easy-going husband, bald and comfortable.

"I'm pooped," I groaned as we staggered out, bags and boxes loaded up.

That evening, we went to the ballet. My treat.

"The last time I was here, it was a noisy, dirty market" she said when she saw the elegant shops and restaurants round the opera house.

We had a snack in the bar and then enjoyed the ballet (*Swan Lake*).

"They came to Joberg two years ago," Elizabeth said, "but there's nothing like London for culture, really."

I watched and listened to the music, but I was tired, aching for something. Mother had gone. Terrible things had happened. Too many people were hurt.

"I'm going to hate leaving," Elizabeth said with a yawn when we got back.

"You seem to have just arrived."

Michael had offered to take her to the airport after taking me to King's Cross. He carried my bags to the platform gates.

"When I get back, I want to have a normal life, Michael."

This made us both laugh. When does a musician have a normal life?

"Be careful, my love" he murmured, holding me close. "Phone me."

"I will."

What I should have remembered was that trouble followed me.

Chapter 28

We travelled north, colours turning grey in the changing light as we rushed through industrial towns, into Waverly Station, under the great castle, City of Burns and Scot. Athens of the North, hadn't it once been called?

We took a taxi up into the hills above Edinburgh, to a hotel I had used for years in Cramond. It always felt like a second home. The landlady was a fan and my visit was looked forward to, a big welcome given.

As I unpacked, the phone rang. "Ms Turner?" a rather tight voice inquired.

"Yes?"

"This is the Edinburgh police here, Inspector Macdonald. We have been contacted by Scotland Yard. We understand that your life is in danger. They have requested some protection."

He did not sound too happy.

"However, the festival is on," he continued, "which means that manpower is limited. Round-the-clock policing would not be possible."

"Inspector, this must be the last thing you need. I can't tell you how sorry I am that you have been landed with it."

"Thank you, Ms Turner. I appreciate your understanding of the situation very much." I heard the relief in his tone. "However," he went on, "I will see that we can do all that is possible."

He gave me his number. "Should anything happen, just ring that number."

Well, at least there had been some reaction from the London end. I wasn't sure if it made me feel any safer.

My landlady, Carol, knocked. "Och, it's great to see you, Jean. How fast the year has gone."

If she knew what my year had been like, she wouldn't be so cheery, I thought.

"I'll be down for your recital. I'm not going to miss it. Dinner will just be earlier than usual ..." She laughed.

I had a rehearsal at five with my pianist. I had some time

Bye-Bye Baby on the Treetops

to wait. I'd go down to the Festival Club. Maybe some old friends would be there.

It was crowded when I got there. I hailed some colleagues and recognised some well-known faces. I had just queued up for a cup of tea when behind me a voice called, "Hi, Jean!"

Turning, I saw that it was my old teacher. "Richard, how wonderful! Are you playing?"

"I wasn't yesterday, but the Scottish orchestra lost their flute suddenly. I've been taken out, dusted down, and here I am. Actually, to be honest, I wouldn't have been tempted if my favourite pupil hadn't been playing tonight. My irresistible urge to hear and see you again overcame my lack of desire to play anymore."

"You used to go to all our concerts and then give us a post-mortem after. How tough you were."

"Good for you all. Well, that was my theory. But, my dear Jean, you have moved far past that. Very proud you've made me."

I hadn't seem Richard for a long time. He had aged. Those piercing blue eyes were faded, his hair white. He had a slight stoop, and I guessed he must be in his mid-eighties. How frail he was. He had been one of the world's top flautists and a wonderful, inspiring teacher.

"Can I monopolise you after the concert, Jean? Unless you have something else …"

"No, nothing. That would be great, Richard."

With still a few hours to waste, I made my way to the Cramond Inn, one of my favourite eating places.

I seemed to have acquired a police officer. He followed me up into the hills, sitting behind me in the bus, walking a few yards behind me down Princes Street as I made my way to rehearsal. Going through the artists' door, I turned and gave him a grin.

I wish I had told him to be careful.

My pianist, John, was already there. We had worked

together all over the world. The last time had been in Carnegie Hall in New York. As tonight's programme was not much different from the New York one, we wouldn't have to rehearse long. The first half was with harpsichord, the second with piano.

"Guess that will do, John," I said, after we'd topped and tailed the music.

Back in the hotel, I had a bath. I relaxed and practiced a bit.

When I got down to the hall again, there was a long queue. "A sellout, Jean," the hall manager told me. "That recording of Bach you did last year caused a lot of interest."

In the green room, John and I waited. I could hear the murmur of voices. John was always self-contained. Sometimes I envied him. I never could stop that pounding heart, sweaty palms, and rising adrenalin. *Deep breaths. Come on, you've done this all before. Time to go on.*

Applause wrapped around us. Only the music now. Harpsichord and flute married together. Bach, Rameau, and Scarlatti piercing the warm air in the hall.

After the interval, I had a new work especially written for me. I could see the composer in the audience. The complex rhythms made me concentrate. There was some Debussy, then Michael Tippett. The audience seemed to like it. We gave two encores.

The green room was a crush of people. An actress who looked familiar gushed, "How do you do it, darling?"

What do you say to that? The composer seemed happy.

Richard hovered in the background. "Let's talk over a meal, Jean."

Princes Street was still busy, with people going home and some on their way to a late event. A few drunks swayed across the road singing.

Richard took my arm. "I'm taking you to the best spaghetti place north of the border."

We went through back streets that had lingering dark shadows. I was glad to be with someone.

Inside the restaurant, the head waiter greeted Richard. He left me for a moment. I sat looking round.

"Richard," I commented when he came back, "this is odd."

"What, my dear?"

"There are no women in this room."

"It's a popular place for gays," he answered.

"Oh, I see."

"Actually, I'm of that persuasion, Jean."

I looked at him. Now he had surprised me. I had never guessed.

"You didn't know? And you don't mind?"

"Richard, why would I?"

He took my hand. "Thank you, Jean. You know, my dear, there was something in your playing tonight—a depth of expression I have not heard before. Sadness even. Particularly in the slow movement of the Bach. You have a flawless technique. And you used it to find emotional depths that were deeply moving. I knew you had something special when you first came to me. Tonight confirmed it."

No glowing reviews or gushing accolades could compare to my revered teacher's praise.

"And," he went on, a small smile on his lips, "the grapevine tells me that romance is in the air. Two flutes. One handsome guy and one beautiful woman."

"Oh, Richard," I laughed. "Guilty. However, not sure. In fact, can I ask you something?"

"Fire away."

"Yes, I'm in love with Michael. He's good for me. But a question always stays in my mind. He's seven years younger than I am. Too old to be my toy boy but young enough to make problems. I can never change that age gap."

He was silent. Then he spoke. "Look, Jean. This will sound corny, but when it comes, happiness should be seized. It doesn't often happen. Most people never find it. I had a chance some years ago. I got cold feet. And I've regretted it ever since." He took my hand. "Michael is, if I remember, mature for his age. So I say stop analysing, Jean. Let your feelings tell you what to do. Go with the flow."

We stayed long into the night. I didn't tell Richard about John. He didn't need that to worry him.

Going out into the cold night, I shivered. It wasn't the night air.

"Keep warm." Richard put his coat over my shoulders. He took me to the hotel in his car. "Goodbye, Jean. Good luck, dear girl. Keep in touch!" he called as his car roared back down the hill.

Chapter 29

It had been ridiculously easy. So she'd gone to Edinburgh, had she? He'd found her image on the library computer, looking at him and smiling at him. Her long neck, like a swan ... How he'd like to put his hands round it and squeeze her life away.

He must get up to Edinburgh somehow. The trouble was that he had no money. What he'd had he'd used up on the car. He'd hardly eaten for days—just what he could steal. He slept on park benches and in doorways, always looking out for the police, the underworld. They were all after him. He knew what he'd done—killed the boss's wife in a fit of rage.

He knew she was sleeping with one of the men he hung around with. Then, that night, when walking home, that terrible rage came. He didn't think. So he killed her. He felt better. After that, he knew he would be hunted. They wouldn't stop until they got him.

How could he get up to Edinburgh then? He had a sort of plan.

One morning he walked into a building society, a gun under his coat. Actually, it was just a water pistol. It looked pretty real, but he knew it would only fool them for a short time.

The girl behind the counter saw his face. Glaring, that one eye, his hideousness clearly terrified her so much that she handed over money, too scared to press the alarm bell.

There were cameras. He'd be recognised, even with a cap pulled over his forehead.

Hurry ... hurry. Get out quick.

At King's Cross, he bought a ticket. He boarded the train to Edinburgh, sitting hunched in a corner, hiding his face.

Out at Waverly Station, he mixed with the crowds. Now to find her. And then there she was—on a poster, her face staring down at him! What luck.

He had no plan. He looked again. Where was the concert? Oh, yes, the Usher Hall. He'd find it. He could wait.

Princes Street seethed. Lorries passed. Cars hooted. People pushed, turning away when they saw him.

In a cafe, he had baked beans on toast and then wandered out towards the castle. That seemed a logical way to go. The streets had fringe events going on, attracting crowds.

He stopped to listen to a comedian. Then there she was, standing and laughing. She turned to smile at someone. He followed her gaze. It was a police officer, a bloody cop. He'd know one anywhere.

Voices in his head screamed. A terrible anger rose, filling and consuming him. He had a knife, a killing knife.

He took it out.

Chapter 30

Bye-Bye Baby on the Treetops

With nothing to do the next morning, I went into town to see what was going on. I have always loved mingling with the Festival Club crowds—that air of expectancy in the air.

It was pleasant in the sun. My police officer strolled behind me, giving me a sheepish smile when I caught his eye. He was supposed to be invisible, but he was anything but. Did he have to look so much like a cop?

The comedian was pretty funny, one of those alternative ones, though for the life of me I never knew what that meant.

Suddenly, a scream came behind me. Looking back, I wondered where my police officer was. Somehow, not knowing why, a dread made me push through the crowds which had gathered at the back around something.

"Let me through, please." There, in a pool of blood, lay the officer, a knife sticking out from his chest. "Someone call an ambulance!" I screamed.

How long it seemed. Under my fingers, his life was ebbing away … *Hurry, please hurry.*

An ambulance arrived. I tried to explain. They let me stay with him as they tried to save him. He was too young to die. I waited in the hospital. There was nothing I could do except worry.

I rang Inspector Macdonald and told him something awful had happened.

"I'll be right over."

I'd wished I would never meet him. Yet moments later, here he was, tall and thin, with kind eyes.

"Your worst nightmare did come, Inspector. And mine."

"Yes, Jean. He was seen getting off the London train this morning. Too late to let you know or to warn the constable."

"I'm so sorry about this. You really don't need it, do you?"

"Well, it's happened. Now we must think how to keep you safe. It seems that you are in danger if you stay. This is a homicidal maniac, Jean, and if this gets out, the press will have a field day."

Homicidal maniac. Now that made me feel heaps better!

"I've found out more. He was in a mental home for a while—by all accounts, very violent. He's murdered before. Now this. This is a schizophrenic maniac on the loose."

Oh God … even better!

"He's clever too. Convinced the experts. Next thing, he murders someone." He rubbed a hand over his eyes "Too many people who should be locked up walk the streets. The blasted human rights people interfere, and who has to clean up the mess, I ask you?"

A feeling of hopelessness washed over me, of a nightmare from which I couldn't wake. The officer's dying pulse was all I could focus on.

"Will he die?"

The kind inspector looked at me. He was faced with a situation that made his job that much harder.

"We'll know by this evening. It's a violent world out there, Jean. When I was a young officer, killing one of us was the ultimate crime. The full force of the law would come down. It was a deterrent. Now crime and punishment no longer go hand in hand, and it says something about this man. He's lost all reason."

I heard him speaking, heard what he said, from far away.

"You should leave, Jean. It's no longer safe."

"I can't do that. I have a concert. I'd let people down."

He didn't agree. I could see that … and I couldn't blame him. I promise I'll be careful!

Easier said than done. Nothing could stop that feeling of being stalked, but life had to go on. Pushing down thoughts of the police officer fighting for his life, I made my way to the Usher Hall. Behind me another officer trudged; he was in civvies but was still all policeman. "Please be careful," I wanted to say.

People greeted me. "Hi, Jean. Great to see you …" and "Good luck tonight."

Bye-Bye Baby on the Treetops

I heard. I moved. I spoke … no idea about what. I tried Michael's number. Just his answerphone … Unfairly, I was angry. I needed him—unreasonable, of course.

Yes, I got through the concert. How heavy my flute felt, my lips dry. Colleagues stared.

I was panicking. I could feel it, a sort of dark morass. Sleep … That's what I wanted—oblivion. And I had made up my mind about something.

"Inspector, I'm leaving Edinburgh tomorrow morning, but not to go back to London.

I don't know why, but something is pulling me—a memory, if you will—a place where I used to go as a child: the highlands."

"I understand, Jean. Might work. But supposing he follows?"

"How could he? Only you will know."

"OK, Jean. Can I do anything to help?"

"Well, yes. I want a car … I couldn't get one by tomorrow. Any chance you have a spare?"

He laughed. "I think we can get one, Jean, and I am going to ask one thing from you, to please an old man. Will you change your hotel just for tonight?"

"I suppose that would be sensible. OK."

My landlady wasn't so pleased, but when I explained, she said, "Och, Jean, my dear … That's terrible."

So I went to play in body with an aching head. In spirit, I think it's called "away with the fairies". Going mad? It felt like that. Cues nearly missed … Was he out there somewhere, waiting for me?

I could see that my fellow players were worried. As soon as the concert ended, I ran to the new hotel. To my surprise, I slept.

In the morning, there was a note at the desk with a key and a car number. "A car is in the car park, Jean. Good luck, my dear. You are a brave lass."

Chapter 31

Bye-Bye Baby on the Treetops

I woke as the sun rose. Over breakfast, I studied a map. I had no particular destination—just to go north and get away, get lost, in that order.

After paying the bill, I found the car, a small Volkswagen, pretty well used by the look of it, and set off.

At seven in the morning, Edinburgh was deserted—just street sweepers clearing the mess of the night before, Edinburgh Castle silhouetted against the morning light, a lone piper somewhere in the distance practicing for the tattoo that evening.

I made for the Forth Bridge and the road to Stirling. Over the bridge I went, carrying on for an hour and then stopping at a wayside cafe for a coffee.

Was I happy to be away? I suppose so. It felt like a fugitive might feel. I was running, fleeing, frightened, and pretty lonely.

A girl behind the counter sat doing her nails, indifferent to this lone female.

What if I said, "Do you know I have a murderer chasing me?" Would she laugh and say, "Och, away with ye"?

I rang the police officer in Edinburgh. "Any news of my officer, Inspector?"

"Aye, Jean. I'm afraid he died in the night. It's now a murder hunt. Scotland Yard is sending someone up ... I'm trying to keep it under wraps from the press, but they're beginning to sense something is up. By the way, my dear, the London inspector asked me to give you a message—a rather odd one."

"What was that?"

"He said, 'Tell Jean to take care or my wife will never forgive me.'"

I explained what that meant, and we both laughed, but my young policeman was dead. I mourned the stupidity of it—all for a man I never knew.

I set off again, the miles slipping away, just stopping for a quick sandwich at lunchtime and then forging o unil 6 as the light began to fall. Darkness falls quickly in the glens. Where could I find a bed for the night? Braemar was just a few miles away; maybe I could make it. Turning a corner to go up into the glens, I caught sight of a notice that a hotel was there. An entrance through a gate that seemed to lead into the hills ... Intriguing. Well, why not?

Going in, I found what was just a dirt track, with only room for one vehicle. Lord knows what would happen if another car came down. *Well, never mind. Plow on ...*

Bumpy and rutted, the track went round and up; suddenly, high above me, I saw a building set on a promontory. I pushed on, coming up to where it was, to find a spacious car park filled with cars. Where on earth had I got to?

Great oak doors stood wide, light flooding out. I walked in. Whoever owned the cars were not around, and it was deathly quiet. It was a huge entrance hall, baronial and full of foxes' heads lining the walls, their eyes watching me as I stood looking around.

Now what? Was anyone here? Just as I wondered if maybe I should go back, a door at the back slammed and a figure appeared.

"Can I help ye?" asked a voice.

A tiny man stood there ... Was he conjured out of the air? I had heard nothing.

"Have you a bed for the night?

"Aye, lassie. Follow me."

We went through another door, across ancient flagstones, up a wide staircase to a first-floor landing, where he opened a door. "Would this do ye, lassie?"

Would it! I had a funny feeling that I knew this room, one of those odd recalled memories, maybe, yet I had never been here before.

"That will do very well, thank you."

"That's guid, lassie." He looked up at me. "I knew you were coming ... It was told in the mountains."

Highland magic? Was he a nutcase? His eyes were

Bye-Bye Baby on the Treetops

deep, bright, and knowing. Had he come down from the glens?

I didn't bother to ask how much the night would be. Somehow, in the strangest way, this tiny man gave me an odd sense of security.

"Dinner at seven, lassie. My name is Angus, by the way."

He left, and I opened one of the windows. In the falling dusk, an owl hooted, and under my window ran a brook—a nice sound to fall asleep to, far from the sounds of traffic. Peace. Hadn't I come for that? Was it here that I would find it?

I phoned Michael. Poor Michael. He must be wondering where I was.

"Jean, thank God. I've been out of my mind."

"Sorry, Michael ... I'll explain when I see you."

"I had calls from the orchestra. They were worried after the concert, saying you were behaving oddly. I was about to get on a train to Edinburgh."

I told him about the murder and what had happened—how I'd had to get away or I would have gone mad. "I guess I panicked."

"All that matters is that you're OK. By the way, rave reviews for your concert. Bravo, my darling."

"It did go well. And by the way, guess who turned up."

"Who?"

"Richard, our old teacher. I'll tell you when I get back. I'm going to stay here tonight, then maybe move on, although this place looks fascinating. It's an old baronial sort of place, probably a laird's shooting lodge, and the strangest little man, a sort of sprite, came down from the hills. He told me he knew I was coming. See what I mean?"

"Well, watch he doesn't spirit you away. Take care, Jean. I miss you."

I had a long soak in the enormous bath, put on a bathrobe, snuggled down into the armchair, and fell asleep. Blissful sleep, with no fear to disturb me ... No one knew I was there. That felt good right then. Everything faded, oblivion, healing ... until somewhere I heard a gong. For a moment, I forgot where I was. *Oh, I know ... it's dinner time.* Downstairs I found a bar manned by none other than Angus.

"Have I got time for a drink, Angus?"

"We can make time, lassie—that's the beauty of being here."

Maybe he was right! Had I found this place because I had to? Now, I am not superstitious or overly imaginative, but I felt something ... Maybe it was this strange wee man with his knowing eyes and air of mystery, how he seemed to know me, understand something unsaid ... Intriguing.

Other people sat around waiting for dinner; a log fire on one end cast shadows.

"What will ye have, lassie?"

"I'll have a Scotch, Angus."

"A lassie after my ain hert."

Neat whiskey. I don't think I would have dared to ask Angus for water or a mixer; besides, it warmed me down to the soles of my feet. Suddenly, the world felt good.

A second gong sounded. Everyone got up, and I followed. Smells of something good filled the air. I was ready and ravenous. I was taken to a table overlooking the glens, which stretched out above the hotel.

I won't make you hungry, so just know that the trout cooked in garlic and Angus steak with spinach washed down with a fine red wine was perfect. I felt benign and suddenly dead tired. A nice couple who had just been to the Edinburgh Festival invited me to coffee, thrilled to find out I had been playing in it. Honestly, I didn't say, "Do you know who I am?" Angus had found out—or knew anyway ...

I fell asleep, waking when the woman shook my arm. "My dear, off to bed with you. It's the air from the glens, you know."

Upstairs I hardly washed, just undressed and fell into bed. Nothing to worry me, no fears, no terrors to wake me.

Bye-Bye Baby on the Treetops

I slept until nine in the morning. Gosh, I hadn't done that for years. I could hear voices outside. A cock crowed. Was that a cow lowing?

A whole day, all to myself. No rehearsal. No need to practice. No phone calls. What could be more perfect? Should I stay? Where else would I find this—what should I call it … a utopia?

Downstairs I had the same table. Now I could see the view. Where else can colours change with the time of day? The glens could be dark purple, then a bright translucent mauve, and this morning a mixture of green and lilac.

Angus materialised behind me. "I hope ye slept well, lassie."

"Like a log, Angus."

"Aye, that's the glens. They do that for ye."

After breakfast, I went out into the foyer. Angus was at the desk.

"Goodness, do you do everything here?"

"The manager is away on a buying trip. He leaves me in charge."

"I've decide, Angus … Can I stay awhile?"

Did I imagine it or was that a smile of someone who knew I would ask?

Chapter 32

Bye-Bye Baby on the Treetops

Outside, the air was sharp and crystal clear. As I stood in the doorway, two golfers passed by pulling heavily laden golf carts. Now that was an idea. I hadn't played for years, but to hell with it. I found the golf shop and bought some shoes, gloves, and a set of balls, hiring some clubs. The starting tee was well marked. Boy, this felt good—even when I shanked the first drive and then yanked the second. No one could see me, and as I walked the course, set in among the glens, I could feel my troubles sliding away. Maybe I was right that Angus was a faerie from the glens and this was a magical place. As I finished, out of the hills came the sound of the pipes. Angus? It wouldn't surprise me!

When I returned to the hotel, I decided to have a bar lunch. There I found the manager, who had returned.

"I was beginning to think that Angus ran everything by himself."

"He could." The man laughed. "If I'm honest, he is the soul of the place, for he was the laird's gillie when the building was a hunting lodge."

A whole day to myself. Luxury. Tea at four, a drink at seven, and then another superb dinner. I was beginning to feel back in charge. Before dinner, I had a practice.

"Ah, lassie, it is as if the angels came down to hear your sweet sounds," Angus said as I had another of his (strong) whiskies.

By morning, I knew I was well again. I phoned Michael. "I'm leaving today."

"Hurry back, Jean. It's been too long."

I phoned the inspector. "Any news, Inspector?"

"Your man has gone. He seemed to disappear. Even Scotland Yard are puzzled."

I knew where he was.

"I'm leaving this morning, and I'll probably be back in Edinburgh around teatime."

"I hope it has been what you were looking for, my dear."

"Yes, I can truly say it has."

I paid the bill, and then Angus carried my case to the car. "Did ye find what you were seeking, lassie?"

"Yes, Angus, I think I did."

"The mountains know. They understand a troubled soul. And your soul was sorely hurt. You came with a burden, and I sense it has lifted a wee bit."

"Yes, Angus, I believe it has."

"Come back one day. Bring your man with you."

"Yes, I will. Goodbye, Angus. Thank you."

Chapter 33

Back in Edinburgh, I went straight to see the inspector to return the car.

"Well, Jean, you are a different woman. That hunted look is gone. By the way, since I spoke to you, I have learned that our man did leave Edinburgh. He hitched a lift, and the lorry driver, thinking something was fishy, rang us here. I won't say it hasn't been difficult. Festival time is always pretty stressful, so I wasn't unhappy to know he had gone."

"I'll bet. I'll try to have a trouble-free time next year."

"Good luck, Jean. I'll call your Scotland Yard inspector to tell him you have got back safely."

I was just in time for the late train back to London. I love trains, so I slept contentedly all the way, after first giving Michael a call on my mobile.

"I'll call round to your house and get the heating going—plus I'll get a pizza." Fortunately, I had given him a key before I left.

"Sounds good, Michael."

If I tell you that it was good to see him, this tall man with a crooked grin and warm, welcoming arms and later making love by the fire, yes, I reckon I could be with him. Come on, woman. What's not to like!

"Now, tell me all about it. What happened up there. Who was this Angus?"

"It was very strange, Michael. He was sort of magical. It must have been that Celtic second sight or something, but he seemed to know I was coming."

"Tell me about the murder. It was in the papers. You weren't mentioned, fortunately—that's why I didn't realise you were involved."

"Well, I'm back now."

"Which brings me to something … My mother and father would love to meet you. Are you game to go down to see them tomorrow?"

"I'd love to."

Yes, I meant it, but meeting a boyfriend's parents …!

Chapter 34

We set off early the next morning. I won't kid you and say I hadn't a care in the world meeting my lover's family.

"Tell me something about your mother and father, Michael, and do you always take girlfriends to be vetted?"

"Dozens, of course. OK, my father is a retired doctor. He retired fairly early when he saw the way things were going, plus wanting more time for his passion ... archaeology. He and Mother have spent most holidays digging on their knees. I used to get dragged along too."

"And your mother?"

"She's a painter, a jolly good one, actually. She also plays a mean trombone. I often conduct the local orchestra she plays in. In fact, I enjoy it so much, I might one day do some more!"

"They both sound interesting." (Or did I mean daunting?)

"Another thing, Jean." He turned to look at me. "Mother is eight years older than Father."

"You knew."

"Elizabeth dropped a hint, actually. Look, if it doesn't worry me, why should it worry you? Oops ... we seem to have a police escort."

And so we did. Good old Scotland Yard.

"They have taken it seriously. You know, Michael, when the inspector in Edinburgh told me that John had probably lost all sense of reason, it scared me more than anything so far. That's why I fled away from it all."

"I understand completely."

"To kill a police officer on a whim—a mad impulse—is so sick."

We had arrived. The family home was in a line of individual rather substantial homes. One thing that stood out was the garden, literally ablaze with glorious colour.

"Who's the gardener?"

"Father, I suppose ... Mother directs with a gin and tonic in one hand and a colour chart in the other."

I rather liked the sound of this mother.

Bye-Bye Baby on the Treetops

Michael tooted the horn. His mother must have been looking, for the door opened and a woman emerged. Well, I say *emerged*, but it was more like erupted, in a flurry of flying chiffon, running down to meet us.

"My dears, how wonderful to see you … and, Jean, how lovely to meet you."

I was enfolded in a perfumed and comfortable embrace. Michael's father followed in her wake. Grinning, he took my had and made me welcome too. How like his son he was—the same crinkly smile, with brown eyes and a humorous grin.

"Come in, come in. Let's catch up with everything," Mary trilled.

"Champagne cooling, as this deserves a celebration," Stephen said.

In we went. If I had worries about meeting these people, it was soon dispelled.

Ideas bounced around, ranging from literature to music, and then I told Stephen that I had studied archaeology, which clinched it … I had his approval!

"Jean, let's go get lunch ready and leave the two men together," Mary suggested.

She led me into the kitchen, where I could see that lunch was already prepared. "I thought we could have a bit of time together Jean. Let's have a glass of wine."

I sensed that this mother wanted to know more.

"I have been sensing some sadness Jean. You don't have to tell me, but maybe I can help. But first tell me, are you from a musical family?"

"No, not at all … I'm the first, I suppose. There might be some way back, but I haven't heard of any."

"Where did you and Michael meet?"

"In the orchestra. He is second flute to my first. We sat next to each other for a long time, until something happened."

"Tell me if you want to."

So I did, for I felt this mother of my lover should know what sort of person her son had fallen in love with.

"Well, my dear, what a story! And how terrifying … You know, Jean, we are not responsible for our parents … The burden is not yours. Your mother found herself in a dreadful situation and, from what you tell me, regretted it all her life—and to find out that her child is involved so long after that must have been terrible."

Well, she knew. Would she judge me? Would she say to her husband, "We can't have a girl like that in the family, she won't do you know?" No, I didn't think so, for she seemed a woman of compassion.

"Let's join the men, dear."

Lunch was in a lovely conservatory overlooking the back garden. This was a loving home. Michael's parents were happy. Looking back, mine had been, but Father died when I was sixteen so Mother had to be all things to us. And now that I knew more about her, I could recall many times when I found her in tears and never knew why.

Listening to everyone talking, I was glad I had told Mary. Whatever she thought, I would accept.

We stayed the night. My room was next to Michael's.

"Only a yard away." He groaned when I said no sex in his parents' house. "You can't stop me thinking about it. Goodnight, my little love."

As we prepared to leave the next morning, Mary hugged me. "Visit again soon, Jean, and let us know about that dreadful man. Take care, dear girl."

"There, I said they would love you," Michael said as we drove away.

Chapter 35

I had Russia confirmed when I got home, which meant a whirlwind of organisation. organising substitutes for several concerts, and shopping for clothes.

"Get warm, thick jumpers and gloves. A player who has been there said you can't imagine cold like they have, and we're going in winter," Michael said.

I hadn't thought about John for days, I suppose purposefully shutting him out, so when the Scotland Yard inspector called, it all came back ... What had he been up to now?

"I have news that might please you, Jean. We've caught your man. It was a bit of luck, actually. A woman was looking out her window and saw a man falling into the bushes in a garden opposite. As it was a neighbourhood watch area, she phoned the police, and bingo—there he was. I'm told he seemed glad to be caught, for he was cold and hungry, giving up without a whimper."

I listened with a relief mixed with concern. He was a poor man, whatever Michael said. He did want to kill me. But my emotions were mixed.

"He'll appear in court, probably next week. It's just a formality. I doubt he will be bailed. He has too big a risk of absconding."

"Will I be needed?"

"Not then. Maybe later. It takes ages. The wheels of justice grind slowly, Jean. But because Edinburgh and Sweden are involved, you may be called."

"He's out of circulation—that's something."

"May I ask a favour, Jean?"

"Of course."

"I'm being nagged at home to find out your next concert in London. My wife wants to go."

"My next one is on December twentieth in the Royal Albert Hall. Please come as my guest."

"She'll be over the moon."

Putting down the phone, I was thinking, *Poor wretch.* Yes, poor John. He was starving, filthy, and hounded by not

Bye-Bye Baby on the Treetops

just the police but also the underworld. He had killed. But he was mad, and his fate had never given him a chance.

I tried to sleep, only to fall into a dream. I was outside the mill. The mill door was open. I walked in. On my right was a room with a bed. In the bed were two figures, a woman and a man. The woman raised her head. Oh my God! It was me lying there—or was it Mother? Her long golden hair was spread over the pillow.

"Jean, Jean, I'm sorry," she whispered.

Beside her lay a boy, the boy John. He too looked up. But now he was John the man, angry and hideous.

"I'll kill you, just wait."

In terror, I backed away, stumbling into the mill. Looking round, I saw something, someone, a figure sitting in a chair at the far end. Drawing nearer, I could see it was an old man, bony shoulders covered by a shawl, blue-veined hands rubbing his face as he rocked backwards and forwards.

Looking up, he saw me. His eyes widened, and behind me I heard a noise. Turning, I saw two figures drifting towards me, nearer and nearer. Behind me, the old man called, "Elizabeth, Elizabeth, you've come back to me."

I could hear a knocking … The images faded, and I woke up from a nightmare, the sort of nightmare where it takes a few minutes to realise it was just a dream. Someone was at the door. It was Michael.

"Are you all right, Jean?" He searched my face. "You've been dreaming again."

"A nightmare, Michael. They were all there, Mother asking forgiveness, John saying he would kill me, and what I think was John's father, sitting in a chair. Oh, it was awful. He was a mirage, yet I heard him crying that his Elizabeth had come back."

It helped to talk, brought me back to the real world …

I had been told that John had been caught. So why did dread sit at the base of my stomach? And why did I think that I still had a part to play?

Chapter 36

Bye-Bye Baby on the Treetops

Before I left for Russia, I had something to do: see Mary, Michael's mother. We arranged to meet in Harrods for lunch.

"A lovely idea, Jean. I can do some shopping."

She was already waiting when I got there. She was elegant, not someone that you could ignore, a face with great charm and intelligence. Would I be lucky enough to have such a person as a mum-in-law?

"How lovely to see you, Jean, and to take the time to get to know each other."

She would be curious, of course. So would I be. One strong point was that she understood my musical world, the world of stresses and ambition, of passion and commitment. So she must wonder, I thought, why this girlfriend of her son wants to meet. These were questions I would ask myself.

"Jean, I think you want to talk to me about something."

"Yes, Mary, and I see like mother, like son. Michael gets straight to the point, so thank you for that."

"I'm a good listener, my dear, so fire away."

"OK. It's about Michael and me."

"I'm all ears."

"I'm conscious that I am older than Michael. He says it doesn't worry him, but it does me ... Seven years might not sound much, but as time passes, it could. Not least having children. And that is a sticking point for me. I don't want children. Is that so terrible, Mary? And you will want to be a grandmother."

She sat silent. Had I said too much?

"Listen, Jean. I won't pretend that I don't want a grandchild, but what comes first is Michael's happiness, and it is obvious that you are so well suited to each other and that you make him happy. He's had strings of girlfriends, but you seem to be the woman for him. As for children, many couples don't have any. However, things have changed. In my day, you married and had children. That was the norm. But I, unusually, did not go along with that. I didn't want children either. I had a professional life that I loved. But then Michael came along and became the joy of my life—and you know that my husband and I have eight years' difference in age."

"Yes, I did know. Well, it seems that this is a repeat ... and thank you for this. Anyway, Mary, Michael might not ask me, so it could just be academic!"

"He will." She leaned over and kissed me. "Know this, Jean: I hope you will be my daughter-in-law."

I had all the answers I needed.

We chatted about other things over lunch and parted with mutual affection.

I will admit that I didn't tell Michael we had met. There are some things that a man shouldn't know about!

Chapter 37

Elizabeth Muir-Lewis

The next few weeks were hectic, what with teaching, playing, shopping, getting visas organised, and finding players to take over some concerts. Suddenly, it was the day before we were to leave.

I spoke to Elizabeth a few times. "Thank God that awful man is out of circulation, Jean. Have a wonderful trip—and let me know if Michael pops the question."

I was still not sure, in spite of what Mary had said. Was I afraid of commitment? Afraid of failing? Yet Elizabeth's words rang in my ears: "Men like that don't grow on trees."

"You're the one he wants," Mary had said.

But was he the one I wanted?

Chapter 38

He knew he'd be hunted. He'd done it this time—killing a police officer. The voices in his head still hammered, confusing him. He hadn't meant to murder the bobby. He still heard the screams, the blood, the feeling of power as his knife sank so easily into the officer's chest, like into butter. In the panic all round him, he had managed to slip away, running and slinking round corners until he reached the outskirts of Edinburgh and managed to hitch a lift down south.

Back in London, it was no different. With no money and nowhere to stay, night after night he shivered in doorways, stealing whatever he could to eat and skulking down backstreets, always on the lookout.

One evening he came face-to-face with the underworld boss whose wife he had murdered in a fit of rage. He had found she was cheating on the boss, and this roused him to overwhelming anger and rage. Seeing her in the street one day, he killed her.

He knew what they would do to him. He panicked, and fled. He ran and ran, until he sank, exhausted, into someone's garden, lying in some bushes as the rain fell. He woke when a light was shone into his face.

"You can't stay here, mate," said a voice. "Just a minute—I know your face."

Handcuffs were slapped on. He was bundled into a police car. At the station, he was given dry clothes, something to eat, and a bed.

He no longer cared. He knew what this meant: Life. Loneliness. Locked up for hours. Shunned by fellow prisoners. He'd murdered a police officer. They looked and saw evil. There was only one outcome for that.

In lucid moments, he was sorry. He'd listened to Jean when she came to the hospital—that things could be different. Well, maybe, but no longer. He'd gone past the point of no return ... Years ago, he'd have hanged. Might have been better; it would have solved everything.

Bye-Bye Baby on the Treetops

As for Jean, was it all over there too? Couldn't he frighten her anymore?

Those phone calls ... She hated them, didn't she? Wait a minute—of course he could call. He had a call a day.

And he knew her number ...

Chapter 39

Bye-Bye Baby on the Treetops

I was ready when the morning for leaving came. Suitcases were packed, passport checked, visa as well, and I had both my flutes. Nothing could stop me. John was safely locked up, and an exciting trip lay ahead. My taxi was due any moment—and as usual, I had jitters.

The phone rang. Michael? Or Elizabeth?

"Thought I'd gone, did you?" a voice whispered.

Oh my God! How on earth?

The voice spoke of terrible things. "I dream of squeezing that neck, hands round your throat. I lie in my cell planning. Enjoy your trip. I'll be here when you get back ... Don't forget me."

I slammed the phone down. I had just ten minutes. I got hold of the directory.

"Yes, we can change your number."

The taxi arrived. I left for one of my most exciting trips with John's voice whispering, "I'll kill you; don't think I won't."

At Heathrow, most of the orchestra had gathered. Michael had been waiting for me. Together we went through customs, passport checks, and then the waiting room to board.

I had found a Russian dictionary so that I could learn a few helpful terms such as "tooalyet" and, in particular, "zhyensheena tooalét" (women's toilet). I didn't want a repeat of going into a French pissoir to find it was a gents'.

Delays over, we herded into the plane. I took a sinking stomach in with me. "Now, my girl, I'm in charge here, and I'll have the last parachute," Michael said, grinning.

We found our seats, and I will say that maybe it was due to the strong hand holding mine, in addition to the light-hearted atmosphere, that I didn't notice taking off. Instead of the white knuckles and sinking stomach, we were up, and I hadn't noticed.

We slept, ate, watched a ridiculous film, and then heard the announcement: "Ladies and gentlemen, we are about

Elizabeth Muir-Lewis

to land. Temperature eighteen below. Quite warm for the time of year."

That sounded extremely cold to me. After all, two below is considered pretty bad in England, but eighteen! Outside, all I could see was snow. Lights from a city flickered in the distance. Moscow, I assumed. Then we were out into the airport and through customs, where a grim-faced woman with no a flicker of humour signed us away.

Outside in the airport welcoming area, a man waited with a sign reading "English Orchestra." He was a big man with a black moustache and a dazzling smile. "Greatly honoured," he said.

Out we went to get the bus. And cold? Yes, bitter, with swirling snow, piled up heaps, and people scurrying by under fur hats and collars, red noses the only visible part of their anatomy. The bus was warm, thank goodness. Soon we were on the autobahn, on the way to Moscow. Passing though small towns and a village, I was puzzled as to why the people all waved and called out. *These must be friendly people*, I thought.

I found out why when we arrived. Across the bus, GREAT ENGLISH ORCHESTRA was written in large letters (the bus driver translated).

Our hotel was the well-known Metropole. I knew because I had looked it up on Google: five star, opulent, and just three minutes from the Kremlin and across the road from the Bolshoi. It all seemed well organised. At the desk were packages for each player, with suggestions about where to eat and information about our rehearsals.

"Jean, how about sharing a room?"

"I'd like that." Anyway, Michael's room had a clear view of the theatre, so I did rather well.

Up in the room, Michael took me in his arms. "Let's have a wonderful time."

After unpacking, we went downstairs. What to do and

where to go on this first night? "They say to ask a doorman for suggestions as to what to do, don't they?" I said.

In this case, the hotel doorman was a splendid chap. He wore the moustache that we would see so many times. His was glistening and beautifully curled, backed by a magnificent gold-tasselled uniform.

"Ah, your first time in Moscow. I am pleased to help. First the Red Square ... must to see. Very lovely—plenty places you eat."

We walked. Well, I should say *hurried* ... God, it was cold! The coat I had bought seemed more like a lightweight covering, and my gloves ... It wasn't long before I began to worry about my fingers. Frozen digits would not play a flute very well.

I could see, in spite of driving snow, how beautiful the Kremlin buildings were. In the wind, the snow became horizontal, our breath white plumes in the air. Footsteps covered with snow as soon as we walked on.

"Michael, we must get out of this. Otherwise, we won't be able to play."

"Yes, ma'am. This is something. Come on—let's find a warm place to eat."

That was easier said than done. Where? We took a guess and walked down some alleys at the back of the square. Muted streetlamps gave little help. Then, just as we wondered if it would be better to go back to the hotel, we came to a restaurant. Looking in the steamed-up window, we could see what looked like local people.

"How about here?"

"Yes, let's try."

Opening the door, we came into a blast of warm air filled with smells of garlic and other smells we couldn't place, and it was lovely to be out of the cold.

A waiter came forwards saying something. We both nodded. Good thing that signs are international!

"Preelyedavwere pashas," the waiter called.

I guessed that was a welcome.

"Better use our dictionary. Otherwise, we might not eat, or eat something we don't want," Michael suggested.

Looking at a menu, I saw what he meant. This was a local place, so there were no convenient translations for the tourist. I think the waiter sensed it, for he dashed away (we would find that everyone dashed in this place), and in a minute, we would meet one of the most extraordinary people on our journey.

The manager had been summoned. He seemed to sort of materialise—a tall, thin man, probably around six feet seven, I reckoned. He had curly long hair to his shoulders and a huge black moustache—yes, another one, but this was so luxuriant that it would win a prize. It was caressed and twirled, a thing of pride. With a bow, almost reaching his knees, he asked, "You English tourists?"

Michael explained that we were, that we spoke no Russian, and that we did not know the food, asking if he could help.

"I help"—another bow—"with the honour. I make a Russian feast, a little hors d'oeuvres of pickled cucumber, mushroom, and soured cream … a little caviar … also our borscht, which you must try."

"I've heard your borscht is good," said Michael.

"Good." He twirled his moustache with much rolling of eyes. "Good. You will say when you are home, 'Remember that borscht in Moscow?' That's how good."

I kicked Michael under the table, for I could see him beginning to shake.

Dishes appeared. A small heater was set up. I had the hors d'oeuvres, and Michael had the borscht.

"Mm, I see what he means."

As we finished, our host came back, bearing a tray with glasses and a bottle. "You try a little Mother Russia." He filled the glasses to the brim with what I guessed was vodka.

"Za vashyezdarovm, ye [Cheers]." He tossed it back in one gulp.

"Better do the same." We followed. I'd never had vodka.

"My, it sure hits the spot," I muttered as the liquid went down.

Another glass ... The second glass made any cold disappear fast.

Our host seemed delighted. "Now you eat more."

Not before another glass of vodka ... I wondered how he managed to stay on his feet. I supposed that to a Russian, this was normal every day. As for me, I was just mellowed—in fact, if John had walked in, I would have just waved hello to him!

All kind of dishes appeared, including coulibiac, a pie with mushrooms and salmon, and a fish pie called *rasstegai*. By the end, what with the vodka and so much food, time was catching up with us.

"I'm stuffed," groaned Michael, "and slightly drunk."

"Not far behind you."

We paid an amount that seemed reasonable considering we had had the drink as well. Guess that was on the house.

"You come back. Ask for Raskolnikov—that my name, after Dostoyevsky character."

We found a taxi ... Michael fell asleep.

"He sleep well," laughed the driver.

We both fell into bed. "Not how I planned to spend our first night," he muttered as he went off again. I soon followed.

Chapter 40

Bye-Bye Baby on the Treetops

Waking in the morning, I had a headache. No surprise. Then I remembered. We were in Moscow. Over the road was the Bolshoi. Today we were to play there.

Getting up, I went to the window. Down in the street, people were going to work, heads up to catch a bit of the watery pale winter sun. The snow had stopped, and I could clearly see the theatre.

"Wake up, Michael."

He wasn't asleep. He pulled me down, and I snuggled beside him. Then I remembered. "Come on—we rehearse in two hours."

I had a cold shower. "That vodka wasn't such a good idea," I called.

"You can say that again … I've a great headache this morning."

"Take an aspirin. I have some in my bag."

I'm a seasoned traveller, but some places are stranger than others. This was one of them. Why, you ask? Maybe because it was alien in some ways. The Bolshoi is one of those places that have legends, where Diagilev, Pavlova, and Nijinsky performed; where Stravinsky and Borodin first heard their music played; where Mussorgsky had his triumph with *Prince Igor*.

As we walked into the foyer, we could not fail to be excited upon seeing posters for "Bolshoi Ballet" and "Saint Petersburg Philharmonic Orchestra" and, right next to them, "Orchestra Anggleskeey."

The house manager was waiting. "A great honour to make you welcome."

Torbjorn was waiting. "How about this? Is it not amazing? Come, we rehearse. We show what we can do."

I had sat on hundreds of platforms. This one was not extraordinary, but it nevertheless felt special. We had rehearsed in London, so all we had to check were the acoustics and a few spots that needed watching. Sitting

Elizabeth Muir-Lewis

in the plush and gold surroundings, lit by magnificent chandeliers, it was like going back in time.

By midday, we were ready.

"How about a bit of sightseeing?" Michael suggested.

"I'd like to start with something."

"What?"

"The metro." I'd heard about this underground railway.

We found our way and went down steps to the entrance. I had read about the "Myetro Fvaryets", translated as "Underground Palace", but seeing photos was no preparation for the real thing.

"This is called Moskovskaya station," I read, "the first station to be supported by columns made of chrome."

All around us were vaulted ceilings, marble floors, and mosaics. I read, "Two hundred and sixty-five kilometres of track, eleven lines, and one hundred and sixty-five stations."

For fifteen rouble, we could go as far as we wanted. All we had to do was decide where to get out, so we took pot luck. The next station was called Sobornaya Ploshad, or Cathedral Square. This was St Basil's Cathedral, built by Ivan the Terrible to mark the capture of Kazan from the Mongols.

By the time we had seen two cathedrals and a palace, we'd had enough. Mind you, the history was mind-blowing in a way.

"Look, Michael." I pointed to a painting painted in 1643. "That's the same year that Monteverdi wrote his opera *Poppea*. That puts history into perspective."

"Yes, my little historian, it sure does. But right now my feet are killing me."

Let's go back, have a snack, and rest—then get ready for the concert tonight."

Evening came. On with work dress, check the instrument, practice a bit.

An English orchestra in Moscow … Normally chatty, the players were quiet. Torbjorn just stayed seated; it was a big night for him too. We wanted to make it good for him.

Bye-Bye Baby on the Treetops

"Ten minutes, ladies and gentlemen."

My flute was cold. I put it under my arm to warm it up, while strings tuned, brass blew, and oboes and clarinets tested ombrachures. It has been called "like waiting to be executed". I wouldn't go that far, but I'm sure there were fluttering hearts and nerves …

"Critics all here," the manager told us.

That, we would prefer not to hear. Russian critics? An unknown quantity. English critics we knew … They were old friends—but not here.

Time to go. Thumbs up. Out the door and into the lights. A sea of strange faces, aliens in a strange land. Our leader came in. Then Torbjorn. We began.

"Good luck, Jean."

"You too."

The programme had been chosen carefully. We began with Tippett's "Serenade for Double Strings". We weren't needed for that. I could look around. Oh my God, who was that in the second row? A man looking … silly. He was round and bald and wore glasses.

They liked Tippett. Next was Mozart's *Symphony No. 40*. The applause began to get warmer. I even heard a cheer at the back. In the interval, the critics would gather round the bar, where the decisions would be decided and minds made up.

The work after the interval was a brave choice, for it was in their own backyard, as the saying goes. Shostakovich's *Symphony No. 1* … Our flutes played a big part integral to the texture … We finished. Where was the applause? Oh God, had they hated it? It began. That slow hand clap, beloved of European audiences. It grew. They liked us! As agreed, we gave no encore to "leave them wanting more," as Torbjorn had said. "Sensational!" cried the manager.

Later, at a party, we basked in "Bleestyaschye moozikant (Great musicians)". That would do.

So the day ended, weary but happy—no dreams,

waking at four in the morning, the clock still behind. This time I did dream. No mill. No river. A platform. Where was my flute? I had to play. Everyone was waiting ... I felt a push. I looked out into the hall, where there were rows and rows of John ... then Mother. Blonde hair floating and then fading, leaving rows of grinning teeth.

"Wake up, Jean."

"I'm coming, Mother."

"Jean, wake up."

"Oh, Michael, there I go again. Why can't my dreams leave me in peace?"

"You've had a tough concert."

"I suppose so. Maybe one day I'll sleep and not dream ... but why you put up with me, I'll never know."

"The package is you, my love ... and one day it will all be over."

I hope he is right.

Chapter 41

Tomorrow we were to go to Saint Petersburg.

"Let's find a Russian choir before we leave Moscow. It's something I've always wanted to hear."

"Me too. Maybe the doorman can help again."

It was a different man—but just as resplendent. I wondered if they were chosen for the size of their moustaches and height, for he was a striking figure in his gold-and-red uniform.

"You very lucky," he said in his dark voice. "My brother Petrovitch main bass in choir of cathedral of Christ the Saviour, not far from Kremlin. You go speak. I tell brother you come. He will be much honoured."

We took a taxi to the cathedral. It had stopped snowing for a while; now we could see the Kremlin spires emerging as the snow began to melt—greens and blues and gold. The snow was turning to slush as we walked up to the doors, which were wide open. Carved angels and gargoyles peered down at us as we went in. Inside was that smell peculiar to old churches—of incense and candles and age, flickering lights barely breaking the intense darkness and gloom.

Up at the altar, we saw a robed figure, his back to us, black and tall against the murky light. Turning without a word, he wanted to know why we here. We explained. "Return at six. Petrovitch will be here with singers."

That was all. Dark eyes curiously gentle, he bowed and left, dissolving into the darkness.

"Well, that was odd. Let's go and have some lunch," Michael said.

We found a cafe filled with what looked like working Muscovites, if their garb was anything to go by: aprons, overalls, rough dried faces, with the gnarled hands of labourers. As we walked in, silence fell.

"Dobraye ootra [Good morning]," Michael tried.

"Zdarov'ye [Cheers]," came a reply.

Smiles broke out, and chatter resumed. "Dabro pazhalavat [Welcome]."

Windows steamed up as bowls of hot fish soup with brown bread were served. As I ate, I had plenty to think about. Michael had done it—had asked me to marry him.

So now I had to give him an answer. I wanted to say yes. Of course I did.

"Go on, Jean." He grinned.

"You're reading my mind again." I laughed. So what was stopping me? What demons followed me? What was I afraid of?

"Listen, Jean Turner. I've never been so sure of anything—and just to say you've got the right guy this time—so how about getting warm in bed so I can prove it to you?"

"What, come live with you and be your love?" I laughed.

"Something like that."

We left to a chorus of people smiling goodbye, and Michael proved one thing, that I could live with him and be his love. I just had to make up my mind—that wayward mind.

"Did you know that I sat next to you for a long time fantasising, with your perfume making me crazy? I fancied you something awful, but you didn't make it easy for a guy. So will, you won't you?"

"Michael, I'll say yes, with a condition."

"Lord, what?"

"That I can get this man out of my life—then we can get on with ours. Is that fair?"

"OK, Jean, it's a deal. I can wait, but not for long ... Anyway, it will soon be over."

I did wish that he wouldn't keep saying that!

Chapter 42

Bye-Bye Baby on the Treetops

We returned to the cathedral at five. It was still quiet. The snow had stopped, and outside the cathedral, it was so peaceful that it seemed the whole world was somewhere else.

Snow muffled our footsteps. We could see our footprints behind us as we approached the building. Pushing open the great doors to go inside, I saw that it was still empty, candles casting giant shadows on the vaulted ceiling like a great ship. Five struck on the cathedral clock. Lights came on. A door at the back opened, and out walked a line of men, black-cowled, heads bowed, filing in to stand in a row facing us.

One of the men came over to us. "You English?"

"Yes, we are. Your brother said to come."

"Da ... deeply honoured. I, Petrovitch, welcome you. Please come forward. We sing just for you." He turned to go back and then turned back to us. "You singers too?"

We told him why we were in Moscow.

"We doubly honoured. Great English musicians."

Back among his singers, we saw him telling them. All ten of them bowed to us.

They began. At a note from the organ, the great cathedral was filled with the sound of basses and tenors, rich chords of ancient modal polyphonic sounds coming from a deep memory of a past long gone. Then Petrovitch sang alone, his deep rich bass voice rising up to the rafters. I felt the hairs rising on my arms. We sat for an hour.

They finished on a four-part chant. We went down to them. They clustered around us like schoolboys on an outing.

"Spaseeba [Thank you]," Michael tried.

I tried, "Preevaskhodniy (Superb)," which caused a ripple of pleasure.

Petrovitch walked to the door with us. "Big honour to sing to great musicians."

"We will never forget it. It is our honour and pleasure."

Elizabeth Muir-Lewis

Outside, it was bitter. The snow had started falling again, this time in huge globules of driving flakes. Our footsteps soon disappeared.

"Let's find our Bazil Faulty restaurant again," Michael suggested.

"Will we find it, especially in this snow? I can hardly see in front of us."

It got colder and colder. Down streets. Up alleys. Where was it? Then there it was. We fell in, our faces burning from the cold, that blast of warm air exquisite.

Bazil, or Raskolnikov, saw us, arms outstretched. "Ah, you return ... Follow me, please." We were seated in a corner. Raskolnikov dashed off, coming back with a tray.

"Vodka, I bet," Michael said.

Three glasses later, plus a meal to never forget ...

"You drink, then eat, then drink—never drunk!" Raskolnikov cried.

Back he came. "I wish you to try caviar ... beluga and sevruga. Very salty. You need to drink more—taste what Russians have every day."

"Not at those prices," Michael whispered. By the time we had finished, once again we were full but happy.

"You are just tourists?" Raskolnikov was curious.

We told him why we were here.

"Ah, I read about this." He dashed off, bringing back a newspaper. "Here, good crit of concert—wonderful English orchestra. We proud you come here. Please to honour us with photo—then you hang on wall forever."

We let him take a photo.

As we left, Michael said, "Odd to think that we will be hanging on the wall long after I have a white beard and you have grey hair. I wonder what our Raskolnikov will tell people."

It was our last night in Moscow. Tomorrow we would leave for Saint Petersburg.

Chapter 43

Elizabeth Muir-Lewis

We were off early the next morning. I had done some research, wanting to find out about this legendary city, called one of Europe's most beautiful. Three name changes, three revolutions. A hundred-day siege, names to conjure: Gogol, Tchaikovsky, Dosteovsky, Tolstoy.

"Not bad for one city."

"Add the Romanovs," Michael said.

Even the street names sounded romantic to our ears: Gorky, Dachnov, Moskovsky ...

Our hotel was shiny and new. We were well organised. Russians seemed good at organising. And we now began what would be the most exhausting trip of my career, rehearsing every day, concerts every evening, receptions at the British Consul, and add sightseeing—until one last afternoon.

"If I see one more museum or cathedral ..." I groaned.

"Let's go relax for the rest of the time here."

On the way back, we cut through an alley, surprised to find shops on each side—tailors, butchers, a wine shop, and, right at the end, a junk shop.

"Let's have a look."

The window of the shop was thick with grime. By rubbing a hole in the dirt, we could peer through. Inside were jumbles of miscellaneous things—old books, jewellery, glass, flags, a mangy goose head, and, at the back, a doll ...

"Look, Michael. Isn't she sweet?"

She might have been lovely once, but now she was faded, with only one eye. Was she looking out at us and saying, "Buy me, please. I've lain here so long."

Then, as we turned to leave, something caught my eye—a flash of colour almost buried out of sight. "Isn't that an icon, Michael?"

"Could be. Do you want to go in and see?"

Pushing the door opened, which gave off a loud ping, we went in. Coming from the bright snow outside, at first I could see nothing. Gradually, my eyes got used to it and

Bye-Bye Baby on the Treetops

I saw an extraordinary shop, with books everywhere—up to the ceiling, on chairs, on every table surface, piled up on a counter, behind which we could see a tiny woman, more like a puppet, her head nodding as she smiled. Now to ask ... but how to communicate?

"Obraz/eekona," I tried. (My dictionary told me that meant icon.)

Which seemed to work. With a shrug, she leaned into the window and drew out the icon. A spider scuttled away as the dust of years blew into the air.

"Why, it's beautiful."

"Could be a fake. Let's see how much it is."

"Skolka [How much?]"

We were doing quite well, for she wrote something down.

"That's around two hundred pounds, not much if it's genuine. Hell of a lot if it isn't."

"How will we know?"

"That's the rub."

"It *is* beautiful. Let's take a risk."

As we dithered, the door opened and a man came in, a strange man ... He was dressed as if for Savile Row—bowler hat, pinstripe coat, rolled umbrella.

After smiling at him, we went on arguing.

"Go on, Michael. Let's buy it. I have a good feeling about it."

The man cleared his throat.

"Pardon my interrupting, but I hear you are English. You are interested in this little icon?"

"Yes, we are, but we are not sure if it's genuine."

"If I may help you, I have some knowledge of icons."

"We'd be grateful."

He took it, turning it over and getting out a magnifying glass to look more closely "See here. You can tell a lot from the wood and the writing. Only an old one would have writing like this. It's genuine all right—and a very nice example. You are lucky to have found it."

"That's great."

"And now you must bargain. It is expected. If I may do it, I would be pleased."

A shrewd bit of bargaining then took place ... In the end, the little woman shrugged her shoulders—clearly amused by his persistence—and smiled at us, gold teeth glinting in the half light.

"How can we thank you?"

"It has been a pleasure, my dear, and to speak English. You are probably curious to know why an Englishman lives in Russia. It has a story. I have a piano shop just round the corner. If you would honour me by calling for tea, and to meet my wife, I will tell you the story." Lifting his hat, he left.

We paid in roubles and took away the icon.

"Let's take him up on that, Michael. I'd love to know his story, and a cup of tea would be nice."

Leaving the shop, we ploughed out into the weather, now getting worse as a strong wind blew the snow like shards of glass into our faces. Where was the man's shop?

Around the corner, we saw a group of shops on a rise, with steps going up to them.

"Maybe it's up there." There was a butcher shop and a greengrocer, as well as a shop selling Christmas ware, its fir tree glistening in the window. But where was a piano shop?

"Look there, Jean. We've found it."

It was the last shop at the end. As we neared it, sounds of pianos could be faintly heard, getting louder as we got nearer. In the window was a grand piano.

"Let's go in."

Inside, a man came over, asking in Russian if he could help, I assumed. As we were trying to make him understand, out of a door came our man.

"Ah, you have come. I am so pleased. Do come in!"

Inside, we came into a rather large grand room. One huge window illuminated the rather dark interior and heavy oak furniture. Under the window was a grand piano.

Bye-Bye Baby on the Treetops

"I see you observe my piano. It is my pride and joy. I bought it in an auction many years ago. I was told that Chopin had played it, which is a nice thought but probably not true. But I like to think so." He smiled.

He sat down on the piano stool and began to play a Chopin Waltz in Ab.

Michael and I stood transfixed. Here we were in Moscow, hearing a total stranger play, and very well, some exquisite music. It felt surreal.

He stopped playing. "Ah, how rude of me to keep you standing. I got carried away. It is not often I have the chance to play to a fellow English."

As he spoke, a door opened on the other side. A woman entered, and here it became even more surreal. With her came a subtle musky perfume, her dress of reds and greens the first thing we saw in the half light, and then the woman herself.

"My wife. May I present her?"

She was a beautiful woman, stunning—black hair wound round a heart-shaped face, large black eyes, and full red lips … Her statuesque figure, womanly and full-busted, seemed to sway in the floating silks.

"Very happy to meet you. My husband so pleased to speak English."

She stood by a samovar on a table. "Please have a cup of tea."

We said yes and sat down on a long sofa. If I said I was bursting with curiosity, it would not be wrong. The man himself was of interest, but now add this exotic beautiful woman … Pretty potent.

"I know the English love of tea." She smiled.

"And now," he said, "I will tell you what I promised. Why is an Englishman living in Moscow. I will start from the beginning. My dear wife is a singer. She has sung many times in the Bolshoi."

"Da, it is true," she murmured.

Elizabeth Muir-Lewis

We were to hear an extraordinary story of how Russia had changed, how his wife's family were sent to the Gulags, never to be seen again. She was left an orphan.

One day she was heard singing by a wealthy man who recognised her magnificent voice. He paid for her to train, sent her to Paris, and after many years, she was ready. To her, he had been a father figure, but he wanted more. She was young, beautiful, and he desired her. "But my Anna did not want this. She ran away and never sang again."

She came over with two cups of tea. I could see she understood what her husband had been saying.

"And where do I come in?" he went on. "I had come to Moscow to compete in a piano competition. I was twenty. If I had won, I would have been on my way. But I did not. And it made me see that I was not made for the top league. It is a tough world.

"So I stayed around Moscow for a while. Then one day I go into a music shop and find my Anna. We fell in love and married. Then came the shop, where we built a reputation for good service. Many great pianists come here to try our instruments."

"Do you miss England?" Michael asked.

"Sometimes. I come from an old Scottish family, the De Veres. My family have a large pile on the border. You see, my ancestors." He waved at some dark oil paintings on the wall depicting some pretty dour-looking people."

"I was the eldest, but living there, my Anna was not happy, so brother Peter took over. I am paid from the estate, quite generously, probably to keep me away, for I am a bit of an embarrassment to them … But tell me, why are you in Moscow?"

We told him.

"Oh my goodness, of course. We were at your concert. I wondered why I felt I had seen you. This is marvellous." He told his wife, who nodded and seemed pleased.

Bye-Bye Baby on the Treetops

We stayed on a bit longer, leaving with a promise to keep in touch. Stewart (his name) gave us a card.

"If you ever return, get in touch. And enjoy your icon."

Two extraordinary people: a man who gave up everything to live his life in an alien country for a beautiful woman, and his Anna, an exotic bird of paradise who gave up a career for a principal.

Almost like a Tolstoy story …

Chapter 44

Bye-Bye Baby on the Treetops

One last concert in the amazing Hermitage ... I managed to buy some prints for Mary. One last reception by our consul.

"A great success," he said in a speech, "and in a country that does not hand out accolades easily."

The next morning, we boarded a bus to the airport. I was ready to go back. I was so tired that I slept all the way. I hadn't thought of John for days. Now that we were going home, what would be waiting?

We got through customs without any trouble. I had worried about the icon, but it didn't seem to cause any problems.

As we took off, Michael held my hand. It was becoming a habit. Flying was getting easier, perhaps because I felt safe with that strong grip.

"Jean ... a suggestion. Let's go and see Mother and Father and tell them we want to marry. Would that suit? Or do you still want to wait?"

Would I? As we rose up into the cumulous pink clouds—a silent, undisturbed world—I asked myself silently, *Do I want it? Is this the man to live with forever?*

"So when will you make an honest woman of me?"

My voice must have carried. When drinks were served, our second violin, Matthew, rose and called out, "Cheers, Michael and Jean. Good luck, mates."

At Heathrow, it was time for goodbyes—a family of musicians going their own way, our common purpose over. I'd had high hopes for Marjorie, who was pursued by our clarinet player.

Martyn had brought about a transformation. Gone was the mousy hair and retiring nervous girl. She was developing into quite a dazzler and even managed to stop Marion's intimidating her.

We were all exhausted.

Michael dropped me off at my place. Not surprisingly, it was cold and smelling like a place that had had no heat.

Elizabeth Muir-Lewis

But it was good to be home, to get the kettle on and light the fire.

I unpacked the icon. Would it still be as beautiful in the dark English light? Taking it out, I laid it on the sofa. Yes, just an old piece of wood, maybe, but painted by some monk centuries ago, who put his love of Christ into his work. The colours were still as vibrant as the day he painted it. How long had it languished among the spiders and dust, next to an old doll with one eye? In a way, I wished that we had rescued the doll.

Chapter 45

As usual, coming back from a job to find piles of emails, faxes, and answerphone messages was a chore—after so long, there was too much of them to tend to straightaway. Anyway, I was so dead tired that I shovelled them away and went to bed—only to be awakened by Michael.

"How about Cambridge tomorrow? Mother just phoned and would love to see us."

"OK, Michael. See you tomorrow. I'll sleep until then ... Nighty-night."

Ten hours later, I woke refreshed. I dressed and wrapped up the icon, for we wanted to give it to Mary, and we set off at ten.

It was a warm day for December, some sun and hardly any wind.

"That's better," Michael laughed. "Doubt I could live in that Russian winter. It feels odd not to be muffled up in coats and scarves and gloves ... I can't imagine how people can live in weather like that."

"I suppose if you're born in it, you get used to it."

As before, Mary was waiting for us, bursting out as we turned into the drive. "Darlings, wonderful to have you back. We want to hear about everything, what the critics said, how you played."

"Now, Mary, give them time," Stephen laughed. "Let's get our priorities in the right order: champagne, then food, then news."

"Calm down, Ma; we'll give you a blow-by-blow account." This was met with groans.

He managed to stow the icon in without it being seen. We showed them concert leaflets; I gave Mary some prints from the Hermitage. Stephen and I talked about architectural finds in Russia that had just been in the news. Then we decided to bring out the icon.

"Here, Mum and Dad. This is for you."

Bye-Bye Baby on the Treetops

Out it came, catching the light, showing the vibrant glowing colours.

For once, Mary was speechless. "Oh, my dears, this is stunning, quite beautiful … What a wonderful present."

I told them the story, even about the one-eyed doll.

"That's its history—doll and all. You have made that junk shop come alive. I will write all about it on the back." She went round the room to find the best place for it. "Here, I think. It will catch the light."

"Mother, we have something else to tell you," Michael began.

Mary stopped. I think she knew.

"Jean and I want to get married."

Mary collapsed onto the sofa. "Oh, my dears, we had hoped this would happen."

"This calls for champagne!" cried Stephen.

Mary sat deep in thought. Something was clearly on her mind. "Listen, both of you. I have hoped so much this would happen. Stephen and I have talked about it. So we propose, if it would be agreeable to you, that you get married here and let us do it. With both of you so busy, and banns having to be read, it might just relieve …"

To be honest, I hadn't got that far! Would I want it? On the other hand, it might be nice to have it all organised—something Mary would probably be good at.

"It's your call, Jean," Michael said.

My first register office wedding had been a soulless affair. I would want more with Michael. I had no mother. Mary was as near to one as I would ever have.

"Thank you, Mary. That would be wonderful."

She beamed. "I will plan it as you want it. Our local church—and have a reception in a lovely coaching inn. We can confer as we go along …"

We had a lovely day with them. I was part of a family, and it felt good.

On the way home, Michael looked worried. "Has Mother

jumped the gun, Jean? Are you sure about letting her do all the arrangements? You know how she throws herself into things."

"Actually, the more I think of it, the better it seems. Mary will be happy doing it, and I won't argue with all the arrangements being done for me ... I think it's a marvellous gesture, so yes, Michael, I'm happy with it all."

Chapter 46

The next weeks were hectic. I had concerts and teaching, with several new pieces to learn. Michael was the same. I did find it handy to have a flautist as a lover—always there to substitute.

Whenever we could, we went down to Cambridge. We spent a lot of time with Mary and Stephen. Soon I looked on them as family—parents I had lost so young.

Elizabeth was, of course, ecstatic. "Good on you. Listen, Jean, I'm flying over with all the family. I'm not missing your wedding this time."

John was rarely in my thoughts. In my mind, he was safely locked up. So it was a shock when the phone rang one morning.

"This is the *Daily Telegraph* here. We are ringing to find out about the killing of a policeman in Edinburgh, which you might be involved in. Can you confirm this?"

"I'm sorry, but I can't answer that." Oh my God. How did they know?

I could see a headline: INTERNATIONAL FLAUTIST HAS A STALKER. MAN MURDERS POLICEMAN.

I heard nothing more, so I put it out of my mind. It was just two weeks before the wedding. Elizabeth had flown over with her two children and her husband, John. Mary had organised a hotel for them. I went on a shopping expedition with Elizabeth to buy a wedding outfit. I ended up with an off-cream coat and a pale green dress, topped with a small hat in pale green. The day came. Soon I would be Mrs Maitland. The day broke with one of those misty days that turn into sunshine.

"There—I told you I would organise the weather, Jean," laughed Mary. She wore a silk blue suit with a sort of Queen Mother coat, suiting her ample figure.

My family were downstairs. Michael was at a local hotel. "You're not allowed to see your bride," Elizabeth had insisted.

Mary and I went down. Just an hour to wait …

Bye-Bye Baby on the Treetops

"Let's have some champagne," cried Stephen. He always seemed to have some on ice. So I sipped a small glass and waited. The doorbell rang.

"That's early," Stephen said.

Why did I feel my heart go faster? *Don't be silly—nothing can happen today.*

I could hear Stephen open the door. There was no talking. He came back looking puzzled.

"A note for you, Jean, and a bunch of roses."

Oh God! I'd had roses once, before I opened the note. "Thought I'd gone away, did you? Felt safe? Don't. I'm not far away …" The same funereal black-edged card …

"It's from him!"

Mary came over. She whisked up the roses and note and took them away. "Don't let him spoil it, Jean."

"How could he …?"

"Don't let him win, Jean." Elizabeth came over.

How had he managed it? He was in prison.

"Stephen, did you see anyone unusual or suspicious?"

"No, just the milkman."

Just the milkman! No one notices a milkman. Clever. But then, John had always been clever. Damn him.

Once more he was trying to spoil my life … Well, I wouldn't let him.

I left to get married.

Chapter 47

Bye-Bye Baby on the Treetops

Sun shone through the stained glass windows, casting myriads of colour over walls and ceiling. Bells and Bach filled the air as I walked into the church on Stephen's arm to marry Michael. Michael was waiting with his best man, the second oboe in the orchestra.

It didn't seem to take long to be joined for life to another person. I had a new husband until death us do part—not too soon, I hoped.

Rose petals fell, and no one came to spoil it. No one had shouted that there were impediments about being married to each other.

Then on to the reception in an ancient posting house. It had all the right ingredients for a perfect day: potpourri, shining crystal and gleaming silver, rolling views from the window. There was Pamela from school, with her patient husband. Richard, our teacher: "Never look back, Jean. Be happy."

Stephen gave a witty speech, standing in for my father ... Yet I missed something. A part of a missing jigsaw. *Was it something for me?* I wondered.

Then Elizabeth stood up. She talked about our childhood, our shared life, how we grew up without a father, how wonderful our mother was. "And my pride in my sister." As she ended, the jigsaw came together.

We left for Paris straight after. "Enjoy yourselves, " called Mary.

Our hotel was the Place de l'Opera, right across from the Paris opera house.

"I nearly played there once," Michael told me.

"How do you mean, *nearly*?"

"Just as we began rehearsals, the chorus went on strike. They have a habit of doing that, we were told, so we were laid off on full pay. The trouble was, it never was settled, but we all had a great time."

"I can imagine."

We had three wonderful days, going to the opera,

dining on Bateaux Mouches, wandering round Montmartre, enjoying French wine and food, experiencing passionate nights of love and passion ... But it was over too soon.

Back in London, we had to decide things. I had my little house. Michael had his flat. Both were too small for two ...

"If we sell both, that would probably be enough to buy something bigger."

But what? Our demands were near an underground, a small garden, a studio for my piano and Michael's harpsichord, three bedrooms, and a decent kitchen.

"Not much!" Michael exclaimed. "An estate agent's nightmare, I should think."

In between jobs, we looked. Nothing came near what we wanted, until one afternoon, when walking back from a rehearsal, I stopped to look at an estate agent's window, without much hope, to see Muse Cottage in Richmond. There were two bedrooms and a small garden. What drew my eye was the "studio."

"Been on the market for some time," the agent said. "The owners live abroad now and are anxious to sell."

"I'll ring later. Let me have details."

Hurrying back, I said, "Michael, I've found our house."

He read the prospectus. "Looks promising ... Probably has dry rot, leaking drains, and subsidence." He gave me a grin.

"I'm not listening. I have a feeling about it."

We arranged to meet up with that agent at five o'clock.

It turned out to be one of four cottages standing at the foot of an embankment. You know how it is with wanting the perfect place, and that sometimes, as soon as you go in, that's the one. This was one of those moments. Maybe it was the smell of polish. They say to have coffee brewing or bread baking ... In this instance, it was polish and the sun lighting up the small lounge. And of course it all depended on that studio. The agent opened another door. Great! It was huge. The entire length of the cottage. I soon had my piano placed, in addition to Michael's harpsichord. Then to the garden ... Certainly small.

Upstairs were two very small bedrooms—rather disappointing.

"There is permission for a loft extension," the agent mentioned.

We told him we would let him know, but I knew he knew. We were hooked.

Chapter 48

Bye-Bye Baby on the Treetops

My sister and family stayed on after the wedding, sightseeing in a whirlwind month. I had not seen Elizabeth's children since they were babies, so there was so much I had missed. Her daughter Helen was, it seemed, a talented cellist. I promised to arrange a Royal Academy interview. Nicolas, her son, still sixteen, wanted to be a journalist.

John, her husband, was a comfortable if unexciting easy-going man. Elizabeth did what she wanted, and he went along with it.

The last day, we all had tea at the Ritz. "So I can crow to my friends back home," Elizabeth said.

John suggested that we go over there for a concert. "Good fees and travel."

"Is that man still around?" asked Elizabeth.

"Not that I know of—probably plotting something."

"Oh, by the way, Jean, I went to the lawyer yesterday. Mother left quite a lot. We will have around forty thousand pounds each."

"That's surprising. She was in the home for such a long time … Jolly nice, especially as we're buying the house."

They left the next day.

By the middle of the month, we had had a good survey, sold both our places, and by the end of March, the cottage was ours.

Chapter 49

Bye-Bye Baby on the Treetops

How happy we were. Too happy.

In a month, we had our new house keys. We began converting the loft. We explored second-hand shops and antique shops, went to auctions, and found a big pine table that only needed some work on it. Curtains were made by a woman who lived in the first cottage, and we found two matching antique wing chairs that needed upholstering. We settled in. I even forgot John for days, so when the phone rang from Scotland Yard, it took a moment to register.

"Bad news, I'm afraid."

"What's happened? Has he escaped?"

"I'm afraid so. We were transferring him from jail this morning. He was on his way to the courts when there was an accident, if you can call it that. We think it's an inside job. One guard was badly hurt, but the main thing is that your man has escaped."

So what had made me think it was over?

"Jean," Michael said when he heard, "we're in this together now. He'll have to get past me."

I should have known. My guard had come down. I had felt too safe.

I began to dream again—of rivers, bitter words, hideous faces of a man eaten up with bitterness and hate and with only one ambition: to kill. I began jumping at shadows when the phone rang, when out shopping ... I couldn't sleep. When I did, the nightmares came back. I began taking sleeping pills.

This morning, I woke with a splitting headache ...

"Stay in bed a bit longer. I'll be back after rehearsal."

"OK, Michael. I'm feeling disorientated a bit, plus I have an idea." I knew he wouldn't like it. "I know where John will be."

"Don't go down that path, Jean."

"Maybe I could face him ..."

"Let the police do it. When I get back, why don't we speak to the inspector?"

"They haven't done a great job so far, have they?"

Michael left. I knew he was worried. I fell into a doze, waking after a dream: Mother wringing her hands and a boy bleeding—falling under blades, his face half off. A police officer dying ... I woke drenched in sweat. My head throbbed. Getting up, I threw on some clothes, grabbed my car keys, and left. Afterwards, I knew I was no longer in control—a sort of illusionary trance. I only knew I had somewhere to go, something to do.

Out onto the motorway northbound, it began to rain, the windscreen wipers with their regular beat hypnotising me. *Keep driving.* Hours passed.

I knew where I was going: into our old driveway. Sheep looked up as I passed. I went over the same potholes. No one was around; it was deathly quiet. Mother had felt that quiet. Parking under a tree, I walked to the mill, footsteps echoing on the tarmac. The door to the mill was open. I walked in. Thick dust lay everywhere, on the floor and windowsills. Curtains of spiders webs crisscrossed the beams, and there were footprints in the dust.

On a table was a mug, steaming beside a half-finished sandwich. A newspaper lay open. A loose poster flapped in the breeze from the open door. A strange mist hung over everything. What was that at the far end? Someone sitting in a chair ... I walked down.

What was it? It was a dead figure—a skeleton stripped of flesh. A tattered jacket clung to the bones, empty eye sockets unseeing and a grinning smile in the rictus of death ... and something else, freezing the blood in my body: a knife. It was protruding from the skeleton's chest.

I heard a movement behind me. Turning, John stood there.

"You came. I knew you would. Where your mother stole my father, where I was butchered ... For years, I've waited."

Bye-Bye Baby on the Treetops

"Who is that in the chair?" I knew, but I needed to hear him say it. "Who's that! Who's that!"

He responded with the sound of a madman. "That's my dad, my wonderful dad. Didn't you guess?" He drew nearer as I backed away. "Easy to kill. He wanted it, you know. So easy snuffing him out."

"When did you kill him?"

"I was eighteen."

Eighteen! Oh my God, living with a rotting corpse—no wonder he was mad.

"I knew you'd come. I waited ... lusted ...," he rambled on.

At that moment, I woke from my daze. I could smell fear. He walked up and down muttering, a hunted animal, but this time I was the hunted, and I didn't want to die.

On my left was a door. I tried to remember where it led. Would it be open? My life depended on it. Moving slowly sideways, trying not to attract his attention, I made a sudden dash to the door. It opened, the lock splintering. Jumping through, I landed in a bed of nettles as I heard a bellow of anger behind me.

Now where? Up the path ... down to the river? I ran on, my legs on fire from the nettles. The path was stony, and I nearly slipped. Where could I go now? I came to the foot of a tree—our tree. Up there was our swing. "Help me! What shall I do!" I screamed.

Did I imagine, and I will always say I did, that I heard a voice call, "Climb, Jean, climb."

Footsteps thudded behind me, getting nearer. Grabbing a branch, I climbed, branch by branch, slowly heaving myself up until I reached the swing.

Just in time. John stood at the foot. Panting with anger and frustration, he began to climb, heaving his big body up. I had nowhere else to go. *Oh, Mother! Did you ever imagine it would end like this?*

Higher and higher he came, shouting loathsome things, so close I could feel his breath on my legs and hands reaching up to grab me. Suddenly. the branch he was standing on broke with a mighty crack. For a moment, he teetered, trying to save himself, and then, with a crash of broken branches, he fell, bouncing from bough to bough, too heavy to stop, into the river below. He put up no fight, not even a cry, as he went to his death, the waters closing over him. He looked up and smiled.

The swing swayed gently. On the seat between my legs was carved "Elizabeth" and "Jean". I was going to live. I wept for John, my mother, and myself.

Now what? Here I was, stuck. Fear and adrenalin hadgot me up. No way could I get down. But hang on a minute ... Was I dreaming? Was that Michael's voice? I must be hallucinating again. Looking down, I saw Michael, a police officer beside him. I was speechless. How on earth?

"Can you get down, Jean?" he called.

"No, I can't ..."

"OK, hang on. We're getting a ladder."

The officer ran off. Michael stayed. "My dearest love, I found you."

The ladder was put up. Now to climb down—not as easy as getting up ... At last, the final branch and I was into Michael's arms.

"John has gone, drowned. He followed me up the tree and then fell into the water. I saw him die, Michael. Let's go up into the mill. I want you to see something."

Was his father still there? Had I imagined it? No, there he was, still grinning his rictus smile. For thirty years, he had sat there, and now he was free once more. Or was he? In my dream, hadn't he called, "Elizabeth, you've come back to me!" What a tragedy.

I heard sirens. "They've found his body, Jean."

I watched as they carefully took the father's skeleton out. Then John's body was put in the ambulance. Father and son reunited, the end of a terrible crime. I hoped that John was at peace.

Bye-Bye Baby on the Treetops

"Michael, I'm so sorry about this morning. I think I was out of my mind."

"You gave me a hell of a fright. After I left you, knowing what you had said about John, I couldn't stop worrying. Then, during the rehearsal, I knew you needed me ... Don't ask me how. When I got back, you had gone, your mobile still on the table, something you never do. So where were you? I rang Scotland Yard and spoke to your inspector. I must say that he was incredibly efficient. I told him where I thought you would be, which is here. And by elimination, he worked out a possibility ... but I wasn't sure until thinking about the stories of when you were a child, tried the tree you had told me about, and there you were!"

"I don't think I will ever forget seeing you—a miracle."

"I wish I'd had a camera. Your face was a study of bafflement, surprise, and relief all in one."

"You know, and please don't laugh, but when John was right behind me, I swear I heard a voice call, 'Climb, Jean.'"

"Strange things can happen."

"And another thing: John could have saved himself. He's lived by the river all his life, yet he did nothing, just as he disappeared."

"It's over, Jean."

We drove back to London. Was it over? I supposed so. Yet why did I feel it wasn't quite ended? Something unfinished ... Why? For John? For Mother? For John's father, free from his long vigil? So I decided. I had ended it. I would give them a resting place.

As for me? Peace and quiet—that was all I wanted—and to get home and have a cup of tea.

Well, wishful thinking.

Outside our cottage was a phalanx of reporters and cameras milling around. When they saw us moving towards us like an avalanche, they shouted, "Did a police officer get murdered in Edinburgh? Have you got a stalker!" Michael pushed and shoved getting into our door, heaving it shut, some of them trying to stop him, others looking through our window ... Michael drew the curtain.

"How did they know?" I gasped.

"I'll find out," Michael said grimly.

I phoned the inspector. "How have they found out?" he asked.

"Really unfortunate. Usually it's gossip in a pub, something said without thinking. Tell Jean I'm sorry—and thank God she's all right. The problem is that she's well known. It makes good copy, always money in it ... I expect she could make a fortune telling her story."

I was beyond caring. Sleep was all I wanted.

Michael insisted on a strong whiskey ... and off I went. "Remember, when you wake up, it's over." But it wasn't. No such luck.

I slept and slept. No dreams. No nightmares. I woke knowing that I could live without fear ... until my agent rang.

"Gracious Jean. I've had calls from papers, radio, TV, wanting interviews, asking me about a stalker ... a murder. I didn't know you had been leading such an exciting life. What have I been missing?"

"Exciting's not quite the word," I answered. "And please no interviews."

I knew he wouldn't give up. An hour later, he rang again.

"I know, I know ... but interest is high. 'Woman's Hour' are very keen, and it's great publicity."

"Not my kind, Frank."

I put the phone down and then gave it some thought. Maybe he was right—not for the publicity but because perhaps I needed to talk about it, for it felt unfinished.

"OK, Frank. I'll do just this one."

So the next day I was on "Woman's Hour". The next evening, I was on a chat show.

"What did it feel like to be stalked and nearly murdered?"

Good question. What had it felt like? Panic. Fear. Yes, both of those. John's face rose up before me ... Poor John.

Had he wormed his way into my mind? Did I still need to come to terms with my emotions?

"Was it a sexual stalking?"

I had to think about that ... No, not entirely, even though during that last confrontation, he had said he had lusted—for what? Maybe to kill me ... Wasn't that a form of lusting. Isn't that how murderers feel?

"Great, Jean," Frank said when he rang. "Worth several concerts, that was."

Whatever it was, I had exorcised whatever it was I had felt.

Mary rang. "My dear, thank God it's over. You were terrific."

"It's the boring life for me now," I said with a laugh.

"Maybe *normal* is a better word." Michael grinned.

"Well, if there is a crisis, let it be a musical one."

I don't know why I say these things.

Chapter 50

Bye-Bye Baby on the Treetops

I got back to normal soon, settled in our cottage, got to know our neighbours, threw a party. I became quite a housewife—polishing, dusting, cooking ...

I was not very good, but I had some excellent cookery books. Our studio began to look like a musician's studio should—a mess most of the time, music overflowing. Upstairs we would have a huge bedroom and bathroom, resigned to builders for the next few weeks.

Tonight we were having friends in for dinner. I needed to shop. "Won't be long, Michael," I said as I left.

Our path ran down to a latched gate. At the bottom, I could see a car parked, which seemed odd, as there was not much room. As I opened the gate, the back door of the car opened. "Ms Turner?" a voice said.

"Yes, can I help you?"

I had no time to say more. I was grabbed—a hand over my mouth—and tossed into the back seat. I screamed and saw Michael running down the path. Too late. The car backed out and sped away.

"Keep quiet, lady, and you won't get hurt."

A blindfold was put over my eyes. "Why are you doing this?" No answer.

Was John reaching out to me. Had he not drowned? No, I knew he had. So what was this? I couldn't see—just listen. Through London and over a bridge we went with no conversation. I gave up trying. The car stopped. The blindfold was taken off. I was pushed inside a door.

It seemed to be in a modern block of flats. I was directed to another door, and this is where I blinked in astonishment, for it was beautiful. Well, at least I'd not been kidnapped by anyone poor. I felt some comfort with that ... intrigued. Looking round the interior, I saw a hallway richly carpeted. On the walls—goodness!—there was a Picasso and a Chagall.

And in the main room where I was shoved, there were rich red velvet curtains, shelves with leather-bound books,

Elizabeth Muir-Lewis

anAubusson rug on the floor, a Venetian table covered with exquisite objects ... Where on earth was I—and in whose flat?

I was pushed onto a chair ... We all waited. For what, I had no idea. But by now, I had a feeling that this was not sinister. Curiosity took over.

A door opened. A man came in. I felt myself regarded. He came over and sat down.

I inspected him, if that's the right word. He was a handsome man, around fiftyish, thick silver hair framing a tanned intelligent face holding my gaze with intensity.

"Ms Turner, I apologise for this theatrical happening. My men get overly enthusiastic, I'm afraid. Let me assure you that you will not be harmed and we will return you home soon."

"You could have just knocked at my door," I said dryly.

He gave a bark of laughter. "Ah, spirit. I am not surprised. I know quite a bit about you. So I will not keep you in suspense. For I know you are puzzled, mystified ... as would I be. So I will begin. I saw you on television last week and was impressed by your courage in what must have been an awful experience."

"You could say that."

As he spoke, it was odd. I found myself attracted to him, even though I was sensing he was probably a criminal. Was that an odd reaction?

At a signal, coffee was brought in. It was served in delicate Meissen cups.

Suddenly, I saw the ridiculous side of the situation and smiled.

"I see you smile," he said. "You see the humour of your situation. Where most women would faint or weep, you smile—a woman after my own heart, Jean Turner ... So I ask you just to answer some questions I put to you, for I need to know."

He got up to stand, looking out of the window. "Last

Bye-Bye Baby on the Treetops

week I heard you talk about your experience with this stalker. You described him in some detail. I believe he is someone that I have been looking for."

Suddenly, I knew who this man was. What had Scotland Yard said? "You don't mess with these people." I think this was the underworld boss that John was fleeing from. I wasn't sure, but it began to fit.

"Let me ask," he went on. "If I am right about this man, you can help me. Last year we took in a man out of pity, made him welcome, and he repaid me by killing my wife."

Oh my God, I was right.

"My wife had been unfaithful, but we were working things out. Little did I know that we had a madman in our midst—and what I want to know, must know, is why. What had she ever done to him? I nearly found him one day, but he got away, and then we lost him again."

"I know why."

"You know! My dear Jean, if you do, please tell me."

So I told him the whole story from the beginning to the end.

"He was happy to go. He was rejected all his life, living with his hideous face, abandoned, living in the hopeless world of the forgotten. I honestly think he never had a chance. Your wife was unfortunate. She was just in the wrong place at the wrong time."

He sat silent.

"My wife did not deserve to die like that. Oh, I think you have guessed, in fact, I'm sure you have, that I live in a world where crime and killings can be everyday affairs, so you might think what is one more? But my wife was lovely, confused." He looked at me. "Do I sense that, in spite of everything, you have sympathy for this man?"

"I have asked myself that many times, but yes, I do. He was a victim of society."

"Even though he would have killed you?"

"Yes, I suppose so."

"You are a remarkable woman, Jean."

"Sometimes a complete idiot, like most people."

"What were your feelings when you saw this John and his father carried away?"

"That my nightmare was over—that John's father could rest. And if I may say one more thing, your wife's killing was a direct result of the past. I felt that deep down John hated what he had become. I don't think he was evil—rather, a victim of circumstance; perhaps in another life, he would have been different."

The man turned to me. Here was a man of the underworld ... and I saw tears. He came over. "Now, Ms Turner, I will take you home. This time no blindfold, about which I am sorry. I will never worry you again."

Just for a moment, I got an odd pang of regret.

We went back. On the way, we talked. This was a man of wide culture, so why did he have the life he did—well, one that I would never understand?"

As the car got near to cottage, the media was milling around again, to my dismay.

"I think it's time for me to vanish." He smiled. "By the way, my name is Al. My mother admired Al Capone, so that should explain quite a lot. Goodbye, Jean Turner. It has been a pleasure." With a rueful smile, he opened the car door. "Take care—and thank you, with all my heart."

Impulsively, I leaned over and kissed his cheek ... For a moment, he held me. Then he left. As the car turned the corner, he looked back and waved.

Chapter 51

Now to get back inside my house. The people round the garden gate didn't know me. I walked up the path to where a police officer was standing. "No one can go in, miss."

"Actually, I live here, Officer."

"Well! Are you the young lady who has been kidnapped?"

"I suppose I am. Can I go in, then?"

"Yes, miss, I guess so."

The first thing I saw was a picture I would never forget: Michael slumped despairingly on a chair. Around him stood several policemen, looking as out of place as officers could.

"Hi, Michael!"

He looked up as if I were a mirage. Then he leaped to his feet. "Oh my God, Jean!"

The two policemen stood up. I knew I would be questioned, but I had liked Al and he had done me no harm, so I told them nothing. Of course, they didn't like it.

Policemen like facts. They got none. Eventually, they went away. The press gave up, and I was back, Michael's arms tight around me as if I might disappear again.

"I thought I had lost you. I even thought that maybe John had come back—all sorts of silly things."

"I thought that too at one point. In the end, it was an extraordinary experience." I told him about Al.

"You fell for him a bit."

"In a way—maybe the attraction was the danger. Anyway, let's have a cup of tea. You know, I've had enough excitement for a lifetime. As the devil sings in *The Rake's Progress*, the tale is ended ... and this time it really has."

Epilogue

Things quietened down, thank goodness—celebrity for a while ... but soon forgotten.

Keeping my promise to myself, John and his father were cremated, their ashes scattered in the river that had their beginnings and their end. Michael and I were back to work.

One evening we had a Festival Hall concert together. When I arrived, a parcel was waiting for me in my dressing room with a huge bunch of flowers.

Opening the parcel, I saw that inside was a small Chagall painting. A card said, "Thank you for helping me to move on. Al."

With no time to take it in, the bell went. We filed out into the hall, and there on the front row was a line of men—large, tattooed, and grinning. In the middle was a handsome silver-haired man.